Be sure to check out these other thrilling titles in our Grave Marker line, available digitally for your Kindle.

Nikolis Cole: The Low-rise Saint by Richard Black
Rock, Paper, Scissors by Sebastian Bendix
Coattails by Joshua Rex
Tolerance by Hal Bodner
Shriek of the Harpy by Sebastian Bendix
The One Who Lies Next to You by Russell Coy
Full Moon in the West by Dominic Stabile
Bottled Spirits by Adrian Ludens
The Dance by S.L. Williams
The Freaks Come Out at Night by Joseph Rubas
The First Suitor by A.P. Sessler
Vampire Worms by Neil Davies
The Source by W.C. Jones
Brain Attack by A.P. Sessler
The Bathtub by Andrew Richardson
The Grimm Reaper by Barlow Adams
Red Blood, White Wood by Rob Smales
The Memoir of Darius Fischer by Ezekiel Kincaid

Grave Markers
Volume 6

Barlow Adams, Rob Smales,

and Ezekiel Kincaid

A
Grinning Skull Press
Publication

PO Box 67
Bridgewater, MA 02324

The Skull logo with stylized lettering was created for Grinning Skull Press by Dan Moran, http://dan-moran-art.com/.
Cover designed by Jeffrey Kosh, http://jeffreykosh.wix.com/jeffreykoshgraphics.

ISBN-13: 978-1-947227-66-8

CONTENTS

A WORD ABOUT GRAVE MARKERS

I promise to keep this short so you can get on to reading the tales collected in this volume. Folks often ask about Grave Markers and what they are. Grave Markers are, in a word, novelettes. They are stories too long to be included in anthologies (which usually average 5,000 to 7,000 words) but not quite long enough to be published on their own as stand-alone novellas. They are published individually in digital formats, and then later compiled into a print collection. The reason why we started this line is we often heard authors commenting that there wasn't a market for those "in-between" length stories and we wanted to give them an outlet for such pieces. And that about sums it up. Told you I'd keep it short. Now, without further ado, I present to you the sixth and final volume of Grave Markers. Enjoy!

Michael J. Evans
Grinning Skull Press

GRAVE MARKER

BARLOW ADAMS

The GRIMM REAPER

Chapter One

Arthur Rosenbaum ran the tips of his fingers around the lid of the bright green barrel, checking, for the third time that it was correctly sealed. His hand slid down the side and stopped on the biohazard sign, where he pressed his palm firmly against the laminated warning. Sometimes he thought he could almost sense a heartbeat, nearly feel another hand pressed against the inside of the waste barrel, separated from his by only a few inches of plastic. It was ridiculous, of course. There was nothing inside by this point but soup. Soup didn't have a heartbeat. Soup couldn't hold your hand. Still, he liked the idea. It was romantic.

Arthur Rosenbaum was quite a romantic.

More than anything, he wanted to find the perfect woman, one who was also a romantic, maybe even a little old-fashioned, like him, who believed in waiting.

Arthur very much believed in waiting.

Indeed, sometimes it felt like all he had ever done with his life was wait, in the fervent hope that he would find this elusive girl—a pure, wholesome flower of a girl who loved to dance, like in a ballroom, not that horrible grossness that those wicked women did at the club, and whose smile was like a mouthful of pearls. However, every time he thought his search was over, he only ended up disappointed. The flower turned out to be a weed, common and invasive, and the smile proved to be merely ceramic, cheap and dirty—like a toilet. He had waited so very long. Even a romantic, a true believer, could survive on faith only so long, and much to Arthur's dismay, he was starting to lose hope. At fifty-five, he was running out of time.

He had held such high hopes for the last one, Molly McMillan. Even her name was cute, warm, and yummy sounding, a name that would not have been out of place on a box of muffins. The woman herself had been just as sugary as her name, possessing a sweet disposition and a body significantly rounder and fluffier than suggested by her profile picture on the online dating site where they'd met. No matter, Arthur had found her personality effervescent and her appearance charmingly cherub-like.

She'd been a bit older than he usually went for, thirty-eight, but she'd had a young soul, admitting over dinner that she still held great affection, even at her age, for Winnie the Pooh. In fact, she had told him she still held a soft spot for many childish things and that she generally preferred the company of children. So much so that she had chosen to become a kindergarten teacher. When she had added, after some embarrassment and no small amount of sparkling wine, that she often felt awkward around people her own age and that this discomfort had led her to avoid dating entirely for the last five years, he had been instantly enamored.

Arthur often found himself uneasy around his peers, as well.

They'd had champagne at dinner. That was the only drink Arthur found acceptable for a young lady. It was generally low in potency, and girls often commented on how the bubbles tickled their noses. He found the idea pleasant. Molly must have been unused to alcohol, as a second glass caused her to blurt out that not only had she experienced little in the way of romance, but that she was, at her advanced age, still a virgin. She had raised her hand to her mouth in humiliation and blushed so furiously at the unintentional confession, turning her chubby face the color of a tart cherry, that Arthur had become even more smitten. She was so shy and adorable that, for the first time in a long time, he dared to believe that this one would be the one, that she was different. Here, finally, was a pure woman, a woman without guilt.

But, of course, she hadn't been.

It was after he had driven her home, sitting in the car outside her apartment, when he had learned the truth. Tipsy from alcohol, she had smiled at him sheepishly and leaned forward ever so slightly to place the smallest of kisses, so slight it might not even have happened, on his cheek before getting out.

Arthur had been thrilled by this tiny show of affection, by her class and restraint. Then, pausing midway through shutting the door, she had bent down so that she was staring right at Arthur, chewing the corner of her lip as if struggling with some difficult decision. A sudden dread had filled the older man when he'd seen the amorous look in her eyes. Then, she had asked him if he had wanted to come upstairs.

She had giggled when she spoke, like it was some big joke. And the way she had said "upstairs," breathlessly, like she could barely get the word out between nervous laughs, it wasn't charming. She had just stood there anxiously, grinning at him like a kid on Christmas morning, hoping she had received the gift she'd hoped for. But it was too late. She no longer looked like a cherub to Arthur. Now she just looked like a fat, desperate old woman, foul and vile, just like all the rest.

After nodding his agreement, he had retrieved a black leather bag, clasped at the top by two wolf heads looking in opposite directions, from the trunk of his car, a beige 2001 Mercury Cougar with loads of trunk room.

Trunk room was very important to Arthur.

He had walked with her, slightly behind, as she'd dragged him by the hand, looking over her shoulder furtively to gauge his excitement. Arthur had attempted to smile, but even he could tell that it had held no warmth, no real encouragement. Yet so eager was Molly, so desperate was her need to debase herself, that she had never paused in leading him "upstairs."

She had said it so simply, as if they might only spend the rest of the night sitting in her apartment playing Monopoly or looking at old photos of her from when she was a kid, but Arthur knew what that word meant. He knew what she really wanted: to fuck, to slam her fat, old-lady body against his until he filled her with his specialness. She wanted to open her dirty mouth and say crude things, to call him "baby," and pull him deeper and deeper into her evil until he was just as filthy and worthless as she was. Just as tainted. That's what they all wanted. To bring him down to their level, until he was just as unclean.

Arthur had felt nauseated that he had ever thought that this one, this slut, Molly McMillan, could be any different than the others. Hiding it as best he could, he had even managed a thumbs-up when she'd suggested that she slip into something more comfortable. Arthur had prepared the room while he waited. It had taken her quite a while—it always seemed to with the heavier ones—but Arthur had plenty of time. When she had finally emerged, now dressed in a flimsy white babydoll, everything was set.

She had seemed more confused than anything by the sight of the black tarp, which had been retrieved from the leather bag and spread out like a blanket on her living room floor. The bag itself was open beside it, revealing an array of blades. Arthur had been seated on the couch with a length of wire wound between his hands. Some of them caught on faster than others. Arthur thought she would have been quicker, being a teacher and all. He already had her on the carpet, stripped of her clothing, arms bound together with the wire before she had even started to scream. He had stopped that with a warning and a quick kick to her stomach.

He had opened a small cylinder on his keychain that contained several little, blue pills and carefully plucked one out and swallowed it without water. At his age, he often needed a little help. Then, as Arthur Rosenbaum often did, he waited; he had waited while Molly cried into the slick plastic of the tarp, while she begged him to let her go, while she asked him again and again why he was doing this. Then, when the magic pill had finally kicked in, he began.

Most people didn't know this about Arthur, but he was a writer. He'd even been published several times, first in local rags, then, as he kept working, even national newspapers had picked up on his art before he became uncomfortable with his fame and turned reclusive. Only Arthur didn't like working on paper.

He wasn't sure where the idea had come from. Perhaps it was innate, like an artistic gift or a calling he had been born with. Certainly, he'd been doing it a long time, since high school. He could still remember the first time, at the drive-in theater, staring down at his high school girlfriend, Tammy Wilson, the plastic baggie that the cotton candy had come in still encasing her head. She'd just given him his very first blowjob a few minutes earlier. She'd done it so easily. He hadn't even asked. She just sort of put her head down there. Afterward, while she was sipping on her soda and watching the movie like nothing had happened, he felt anger rising inside him.

Tammy just sat, laughing at the funny parts, smacking her lips as she ate popcorn, the same lips that had been on him, on his dirty part, a few minutes before. Who could go on? What kind of whore could eat with that same filthy mouth?

He had wanted her to stop using that dirty hole, to stop laughing, stop eating, stop breathing. It had taken longer than he had expected. Arthur could still remember her screams, muffled inside the bag, partially drowned out by the sound of people laughing at the movie, Tammy's eyes swollen with fear, her face looking like some enormous goldfish that had grown too big for its bowl. After she died, Arthur had looked down at her for a long time.

During the struggle, her blouse had ripped open, exposing the smooth skin of her breasts and tummy. She seemed so normal, so bare. It wasn't right. There was no indication that she was anything other than the innocent, wonderful girl she had seemed to be before their trip to the drive-in. Arthur knew better, however, and he wanted others to know as well. Grabbing the key from the ignition, he'd dug it into her, scratching and gouging until he had carved a single crude, bloody word into the space between her breasts: Slut.

It had started small like that, with short, ugly words. Looking back, Arthur was actually quite embarrassed by how amateurish his early work had been. With each new girl, though, he got a little bit better, a little more precise. By thirty, he could manage sentences. At forty, paragraphs were within his grasp. Now, he had evolved past even that.

Fairy tales and fables held a special place in Arthur's heart and had since he was quite young. They reminded him of sweet, happy things. By the time Molly McMillan passed out for the first time, she had nearly the entire story of Hansel and Gretel—the real one, where the house was plain bread and the mother was mean and died at the end—scrolling around her body in neat, impossibly small letters After that, he worked even more rapidly without the added difficulty of her moving, switching tools as needed, big blades for hard lines, small ones for detail and scalloping. He used her lingerie, a tasteful piece as such things went, like blotting paper, soaking up the blood so that he could keep his writing exact and perfectly distinct. Skin was a difficult medium, but Arthur was well-practiced and his carved calligraphy was immaculate, each letter a perfectly dug-out pool filled with red.

She woke up again, crying in agony, when he reached her inner thighs, and by the time he made it past her left knee, she was so weak from blood loss that she was doing little more than gasping.

Arthur knew about shock; he wasn't an uneducated man. One did not become a sanitation manager by being stupid. He understood the processes the body underwent before death, understood them far better than most. Still, he liked to think of this quiet time as a moment of realization, of redemption.

When he had only a few sentences left, he would ask them if they understood why he had to do it. Sometimes, the really stubborn ones would start with the screaming again, or worse, they'd start crying. Molly wasn't that stubborn. She said nothing, just blew out progressively more shallow breaths and kept her eyes on Arthur's knife. In the soft light of her living room, covered in perspiration and trembling, she looked smaller again, not so fat, and young once more, like a frightened little girl. He called it "The Revealing." They all revealed in the end. She was ready.

As was Arthur's way, he brushed her hair out of her face and kissed her forehead. Then he held her hand, interlaced his fingers with hers. When he spoke it was soft and gentle, understanding even.

"You didn't mean to be a bad girl. You were good once. I can see it, underneath all of that filth. We just have to find it. We can find your goodness. Then you can be free. Would you like that?"

Molly nodded weakly. They almost always agreed by this point.

"What are little girls made of?

Molly didn't answer, but he could see the guilt waiting in her eyes. Arthur could always see the guilt. It was like he was especially attuned to it.

"What are little girls made of?"

She tossed her head feebly from side to side, frustration and delirium warring on her face. Arthur could see tears welling in her eyes. He knew that if she started that, she'd be lost for good, so he led her.

"Sugar and spice and everything nice. That's what little girls are made of…What are little girls made of? Sugar and spice and everything nice. That's what little girls are made of."

Silence.

"What are little girls made of?" He grabbed her chin in one hand and held her steady. "What are little girls made of?"

"Sugar…" was the faint reply.

"And?"

"Spice."

"And?"

"Everything nice."

"That's what little girls are made of. Again. What are little girls made of?"

"Sugar and spice and *mumble* nice."

"Everything nice. Keep saying it. What are little girls made of?"

"Sugar and spice and everything nice…"

"That's what little girls are made of. Say the whole thing. What are little girls made of?" Arthur's words were velvety and rhythmic, tender and soft. They bounced quietly off each other, springing from syllable to syllable.

She repeated it once, perfectly. Then again. He encouraged her to keep saying it. After a few minutes, she was babbling right on cue. It droned on, becoming almost a chant, a mantra, which is exactly what Arthur wanted. The next part was the most difficult and would demand much of both him and the girl. Better that she had something to distract her, something to focus on other than the pain. It was unfortunate, but true artistry demanded suffering and, sometimes, a little blood. Other times it demanded a lot.

He cut into Molly's sternum, right where her ribs made an "A" shape, this time deeper than he had gone with his lettering. Quite a bit deeper. He had left a space for it, beneath the part where Hansel tricked the witch with the bone of a dead child so that she would think him still too thin to eat. The words were garbled for a second, lost in the sudden intake of breath, obscured by the croaking sound she made. But she recovered quickly, sticking to the pattern.

"Sugar and spice and—ahhh—everything nice. That's what little girls are made of."

When the entry was fully formed, Arthur put his hand on her torso, felt the outline, like an arrow of red pointing the way forward, inward, onward. He pushed with his fingers, gently at first but with increasing pressure. Untethered, thanks to his incision, her skin surrendered to his advances. Reaching into her, he felt the warmth of her cavity envelop his hand. She was hot and viscous and ripe with the essence of origin. The truth welled up in her, spread beyond her borders, cascaded down the sides of its vessel. He would not have long to find it.

"Sugar an—ahh!—spice and everything nice. That's what little girls are made of. Sugar and spice and everything nice. That's what little girls are made of." The words came fast now, popped out between sharp breaths.

Arthur searched her vigorously but with meticulousness. It wouldn't benefit him to become careless in his excitement. What he was seeking was rather small, difficult to find under any circumstances. With the time constraint, it would have been nearly impossible for anyone less experienced, less dogged in his pursuit. Arthur was a wrangler of such things, however; he was at home elbow-deep in the obfuscations of life.

She was getting jerky now, spastic in her attempt to escape the reality of the hunt. "Sugar…spice…everything…and everything nice. That's what little girls are made of." They often did it at the end. It wouldn't help. It was too late. He'd already laid a finger on it. Just the tip, but it was enough. Arthur could feel it now, wild and wiggling: Molly's soul.

"Sugar and spice, sugar and spice, sugar and spice—" Into the throes, she was fighting hard for it, convulsing on the floor like some great, pale fish. It wasn't uncommon. This part frequently reminded Arthur of when he'd fished for "striper" with his dad, the way they'd turn this way and that, frantically darting about hoping to catch you on a stump or snap your line. Bass were stupid. Frequently, they'd just end up making the whole thing worse, come out of the water sporting a broken mouth and shredded gills. Girls were sometimes a lot like fish. Molly was. In her thrashing, she ripped the opening wider and more of her than need be gushed out onto the tarp.

Souls were fast little devils, tricky, and while they weren't exactly smart, they were cunning, just like those striped bass. This one was an especially devious one, and it darted back and forth, leading Arthur this way and that. On a lesser angler, it might have worked, but Arthur was seasoned. He knew when to zig, when to zag, and he kept his hand firm enough to be secure but loose enough not to get caught bearing down and lose it. The back of his hand pushed against the inside of Molly's skin, and he could see the outline of his knuckles pressing up when he entered the cramped area. He stayed patient, let the soul tire itself out. Let it run. There was a bit of splashing and only the faintest gasps and a murmur of a single word.

"Sugar…sugar…sugar."

With one last gambit, Molly's soul tucked in on itself, end-to-end, and shot straight up into her chest through the narrow path. In the early days, that might have been enough to get free, but now Arthur knew simply to follow, which he did, jerking his hand past the lungs, right up to the heart, fast enough and hard enough that he heard the cracking of ribs.

It was the last sound Molly McMillan ever made. There were no more gasps. No more repeating of rhymes. No more anything.

Arthur didn't notice. He had his catch.

Gently and slowly, he brought it forth, out of her sternum and up to his face, his fist still clenched around it. A lot of people wouldn't have been able to see it, might have even argued that it wasn't there, but to Arthur it was a glowing light radiating through the cracks in his fingers, so bright and so pure that, even partially blocked, it forced him to squint just to look at it. Still, he had to check; they were all different.

With one hand clasped over the other, he made a sort of tunnel with the areas between his thumbs and index fingers, then, pressing one eye to the end of the tunnel, he gradually relaxed his grip enough so that he could see her soul, which he examined gleefully and with great fascination, like a child who had captured a firefly.

He was not disappointed. Molly's soul was an exceptional specimen, shiny, so shiny in parts that it threatened to blind him, and warm and white, like radiant milk. There was no tarnish—Arthur attributed this to her virginal status—and it almost hummed with untapped energy. It had been a long time since he had seen its equal.

So close. She had been so close.

Feeling momentarily sad, Arthur spared a glance to the wrecked body he had pulled it from. It was exposed now, open and empty, like a lake that had been dredged and left to dry in the hot summer sun of her living room lamplight. She had been pretty, hadn't she? Cute? It seemed as if she had been. It was hard to remember. He almost missed her liveliness for an instant. He felt, well, not guilt, but something close —almost guilt, the way someone feels when one remembered how perfectly shaped an egg had once been before they cracked it open to make an omelet.

Then he remembered the way she had said "upstairs," and the almost-guilt disappeared. A disgusted look crawled across his face, and he forced himself to stay happy in the moment. It was such a special moment for Arthur. He focused once more on the precious treasure in his hand. No, far better that he had removed such a wonderful gift from its unworthy shell. Far better to eat the omelet.

He tightened his grip.

Arthur sat on the couch and carefully unbuttoned his pants with the hand not holding the soul, careful when sliding them down not to get any of the splatter clinging to them on the couch. Underwear followed, tight and white and now spotted with red. The Viagra was still working its magic, and his excitement sprang up as soon as his briefs came off. With great deliberateness and care, he brought his fist parallel to his arousal, and then, in a quick but controlled manner, efficient and tight to keep the soul from escaping, he wrapped his bloody fingers around his manhood, trapping the glowing brightness against his sex.

Slowly, at first, he began to touch himself. The slickness from the blood helped, and the heat from Molly's soul sent tingles through his body. More than at any other time, Arthur felt right, basking in the shaky illumination of that soothing light. Each stroke sent rays of it bouncing across the room, across him, across what had been Molly. They all seemed connected in that purifying glow, all of them perfect, all of them fresh and new.

Happiness spread through him from that spot of contact with the soul, swam in his veins, up his body, down his legs, fluttered his heart before emerging from his throat in a long, droning satisfied moan—a joyful, peaceful, contented sound. Just as quickly, it fell back down his esophagus, climbed up his legs and into his groin.

Happiness shot from him, an explosion of it, and Arthur reveled in the slick warmth on his hands, the play of light, the reaffirming sound of his own achievement. Desperately, he wanted to make it last, and he milked it firmly and rigorously until happiness barely leaked from him, and then ceased to drip at all.

Opening his hand, he saw the crimson-smeared skin of his penis, more pink now combined with his happy mixture, but no light. It had been extinguished in the rubbing. It always was.

This was the hardest part: the death of that sweet light, snuffed out like a fairy, a flying little beam of hope.

Arthur Rosenbaum hated when he thought of them like fairies. He was quite fond of fairies, and seeing the little souls in that way, well, it made him sad.

Arthur was quite tender-hearted, and he showed it by sitting on the couch, naked and streaked with blood, and crying softly over the death of what had never been a fairy, in an apartment that had once been Molly McMillan's.

Nothing would be Molly's again. Not even her soul. It was Arthur's now, just another winged memory—a happy thought.

Chapter Two

When he was through mourning the fairy that wasn't a fairy, he dressed and went about concluding the ritual.

Everything had a point, a place. An artist had to clean up afterward. Sloppy clean-up led to fame and newspapers, and Arthur no longer courted that kind of mainstream appeal. They would start calling him that name again. The one he hated.

It would be enough if he alone knew. Art for art's sake. That was the truest expression.

He showered in her bathroom, noticing as he did the hasty way she had left her own clothing strewn on the floor. He sneered once more at her hurry to debase herself. Strange that one so whorish had contained such a beautiful glow.

When he was finished, he used the cleaning supplies in his bag to thoroughly scrub everything: the shower, the carpet—everything. Oxiclean, he found, was as good as anything. Sham Wows, too.

Arthur had trouble sleeping sometimes, and often found himself watching late-night infomercials. Contrary to what most people thought, the products were generally top-notch and could handle most any job, no matter how messy. Just like the enthusiastic gentlemen on the television said they would. A portable Dirt Devil sucked up anything he had missed.

Pausing, Arthur knelt over the former Molly one last time. Not to mourn, or grieve, but rather to read. He traced his fingers from the first line, Next to a great forest there lived a poor woodcutter with his wife and his two children. The boy's name was Hansel, and the girl's name was Gretel. He had but little to eat, and once, when a great famine came to the land, he could no longer provide even their daily bread. It started behind her left ear and ended at the middle of her neck, all the way to, My tale is done. A mouse has run. And whoever catches it can make for himself from it a large, large fur cap. Which ended with a firm period on her right calf.

When finished, he made a satisfied noise, then rolled her body up, making sure to fold the tarp as he did in a manner that ensured the blood would stay neatly packaged with the body and prevent any unsightly spills. Even Oxiclean had its limits.

A casual walk to his car proved uneventful. In his experience, Arthur found that people in movies and on television tended to greatly exaggerate the need for stealth. Most people simply didn't care what you were doing unless you advertised it. Acting like you belonged went an awfully long way, he had found. All of the way, in most instances. A well-placed fib usually covered any additional ground required. Few would pursue it any further. It turned out people liked watching shows about being perceptive and investigatory far more than doing the actual leg-work.

There was no furtive drive to where he worked at the garbage site, either. Arthur drove the speed limit, even a bit over it at times, with the windows down and Frank Sinatra's "Young at Heart" blaring out into the night. The world didn't know what he had in the trunk of his car. The world didn't care.

His key unlocked the gate at the dump, and a code let him into the area where the toxic waste was disposed. He was careful that the barrels were always properly sealed and that the coded numbers always matched, always came in the right order. After that, it took just a bit of strength and remembering to lift with his legs for Arthur to have what used to be Molly floating indelicately in the vat of medical waste that was to be buried the next day, her hand perhaps pushing somewhere on the other side of the thick opaque plastic. The biohazard sign on the side of the barrel would do most of the work; human indifference would do the rest. Another can of soup into the ground, a remembered moment of warmth for Arthur, a ration for a rainy day.

When the headlights of his Mercury finally kicked back on, the results of his date were sealed in only a single barrel among many, no different than any other apart from the particular string of numbers and letters that ran around the top.

Nobody said goodbye to him as he exited the dump. No one cheered as he relocked the gate and drove off into the last hours of Friday night. There was no fanfare for the departing writer. Another project completed, another heroic deed accomplished, and the world went on sleeping, unaware of how it benefitted from the genius of Arthur Rosenbaum.

Arthur didn't like to use the word "hero" when referring to himself, but, he had to admit, that it sort of fit. It was a thankless job, creating art, purifying the corrupt. But where would the world be without him? These women—he hesitated to call them that—would just be running around, spreading their sin, their filth.

No, they weren't like women at all, not the way women were supposed to be: innocent, pure, modest, and sweet. They were more like a disease, a plague of locusts gobbling up anything they could get their hungry, dirty little mouths on. Arthur knew what they wanted in those mouths, and it made him sick.

Locusts, that's what they were. And he was like a spider. No one ever appreciated spiders because sometimes, in going about their important work helping to cull unwanted elements, they could look a little scary to the uninformed. But Arthur wasn't scary. He was really very nice—a nice, well-meaning spider spinning his web of words.

Oooh, like Charlotte, from *Charlotte's Web*! Yes, a spider, that's exactly what he was. He very much liked that idea, and drove for some time, thinking, smiling, imagining people gathering around to see his words suspended in skin the way that the heroic Charlotte's had been suspended in silk. He was just trying to save people, too, but from themselves. If he could find a woman like Wilbur—well, not as fat as Wilbur, preferably, but Arthur was willing to make concessions—he and she would be happy, just like in that novel. She would be good of heart, just like that "special pig," and would be unburdened by all of that awful guilt that the women he met carried around.

This idea filled Arthur with joy. Despite everything, all his failed searching, he still believed wholeheartedly in fairy tales, in happy endings. And he wanted so passionately to be a character in one of his beloved children's stories, but he could never decide which one. Maybe Charlotte was his character. Oh, how he loved those stories. You could learn all there was to know about life from a children's story. Arthur believed that. Completely.

It wasn't until later in the drive that he remembered something that caused him to rethink his sudden association with the beloved arachnid from that most famous of books: Charlotte died at the end.

Chapter Three

When driving home from work, Arthur generally took the shortest route and was usually at his house within ten minutes. One of the reasons he had selected the quaint, little, two-bedroom ranch was precisely because of its proximity to the dump—a feature that, for most, made the property less desirable and lowered the asking price a bit. The neighbors often complained about the smell, which you could catch very clearly on the autumn breeze if the wind shifted and you stood in exactly the right spot on his porch. Arthur knew this spot well. Truth be told, he often sought it out, purposely standing there, sometimes for the better part of an hour, letting that rancid odor waft up his nostrils. For most, the smell brought merely revulsion, but for Arthur, it brought memories, old stories, some he had written long ago when he first started working at the site almost thirty years ago, blowing back to him. That rancid smell was a library to him, and he perused it lovingly. He was smelling the odor of his life. Arthur couldn't get enough of the scent.

For this same reason, after making a drop-off, he would always take a different, much longer way home, down Old River Road. It ran around the dump in something of a circle. Well, an oval now. As the dump had grown too large for its original confines, new zoning had been commissioned and new land bought, and it had expanded significantly on its eastern side, making the site something of an oblong shape. The road had been moved and repaved accordingly.

Why it was called Old River Road, Arthur was unsure, as the creek that dribbled along was nothing resembling a real river, nor was it very old. It was just a wretched, little run-off, really, like the dark water that came from his gutters after a good cleaning, a dank, little ditch that sometimes filled with refuse and rainwater and circled the dump like a stagnant moat. This was befitting the great mound of garbage that, in his mind, he had taken to calling "The Glass Castle," in reference to its height and the way the sunlight often played off the generous littering of glass bottles and reflective bits of metal.

There were even sentinels from time to time, crows and scavenging birds that would man the battlements and call out warning cries to each other when intruders, the sanitation workers, would approach. Arthur liked this idea. Many of the best fairy tales featured castles, often a prince, or a dragon that billowed out smoke—much like the great incinerator on the north side did, like a great sleeping beast that hoarded garbage. Most dragons preferred treasure, but what was it that they said about one man's trash? Maybe this dragon was fond of aluminum cans and bottle caps.

Many such stories involved a bewitched princess, a sleeping beauty.

This one, his tale, featured several sleeping beauties.

They called to him as he drove around the winding, little road parallel to the sputtering drainage creek. He knew it was silly, but as he entered each new section, he could have sworn that he smelled the scent of each woman: Meredith, who had been a dance instructor, and her faint scent of baby powder, treatment for the way her thick thighs had chafed when she moved; Abigail, and the spicy smell of chilis that always clung to her hair after she got off her job at Chipotle; Sue, with her constant chewing of her too strong wintermint gum to hide the sweet decay of her halitosis.

It should have been quite impossible—of that he was sure—like picking out the scent of one overly ripe banana over the combined stink of a thousand. Still, some part of him insisted that it was true, that he could differentiate them, entombed as they were beneath several tons of compacted refuse. He was attuned to them, to the smell of his accomplishments and the stench of their failures. He could smell them, just like he could see the souls.

Each one was different, a unique shade, a definitive brightness, some cracked and tarnished, others nearly right, like Molly's had been. All of them, however, had been ultimately flawed. If he were being honest, he would have admitted that he remembered the little balls of light more clearly than he did the women—the way that they had felt against his skin, how they had made him happy, the way they had eventually winked out.

They were all imitations. False princesses. They would never have been able to get their fat, ugly feet into the glass slipper. But there was one out there who would, and she would be pure like Snow White, beautiful like Belle, and adventurous like Ariel. He would know her, she would know him, and they would dance on air. Her soul would shine a brilliant, undiluted white, and it would never wink out, no matter how hard he rubbed.

And Arthur wouldn't even need to take hers out to feel it. He'd be able to see it glowing in her chest and feel it, warm and soothing even through her skin, so hot that no polyethylene barrel could block out the heat.

He was so focused on the idea of her that he almost missed the actuality of her.

The tail end of his way home always took him past the old elementary school, which had been shut down decades ago. The children, more specifically the children's parents, didn't seem to have the same affinity for the garbage smell. And there were health concerns about the smoke from the incinerator and the runoff from the creek. The dump was no place for innocents.

He barely ever noticed the school anymore. It was hard to see, even under a moon that was as full and pale as a well-fed tick, half-shrouded by the nearby woods that grew thick around the mountain of refuse. Gray limbs, twisted and thick from supping on the putrid strength of the runoff from the creek, obscured most lines of sight. Barely visible through the tangle, the old yard had stood empty for so long, just a ramshackle building and the skeletal remains of a playground. Even the crows that seemed to nest and perch everywhere near the trash site avoided it. No crumbs in a graveyard.

It was the color that drew Arthur's attention. A bright red, streaking forward before disappearing behind a tree a second later. He thought he imagined it--surely nothing so vibrant could live in such a gray, lifeless place—but it reappeared an instant later and then vanished once more, just as quickly. It took him a minute to figure it out: someone was playing on one of the old swings.

The gravel driveway into the school had long since been overgrown, but with care, Arthur managed to maneuver his car along the bumpy path. Peering through the trees as he steered, he kept his focus on the crimson flare. It was almost like a fishing lure, jigging back and forth under the shadow of The Glass Castle. Arthur swam after it readily.

Eventually, the car circumvented the cover of the trees and the driveway meandered into what was once the parking lot but was now a grassy, spongy field. Free from obstacles, Arthur just sat in the car and watched the swinger from the comfort of his vehicle.

Though he had pulled fairly close to the playground, the girl on the swing gave no sign she recognized his presence. She was young, in her early twenties probably, but dressed to look even younger in a loose-fitting, plain, white t-shirt and a pair of jean shorts with a flower design on one leg, rolled up to the upper portion of her thigh. Over the top of this, she wore a neon red, synthetic windbreaker, unzipped in the front. Her hair was a dirty blonde, the color of dry mustard, and pulled into pigtails. A pair of worn sandals flapped about on her feet, threatening to fly off with every swing. Her feet, which were encrusted with dirt, probably from walking in the woods, peeked through the old leather straps. She wiggled her toes at the apex of her swings as if she were having the most fun she had ever had.

She still gave no indication that she noticed him or his vehicle.

Arthur immediately liked her.

Arthur stopped the engine but left the headlights on so that he could see. Getting out of his car, he slammed the door hard, hoping that the noise might cause her to acknowledge him. When it didn't, he stood awkwardly, unsure of how to proceed. He must have stood there silently for the better part of five minutes, shuffling his feet, casting a long shadow in the glare of the Mercury's lights.

He didn't always know what to say to people. First lines were the worst. Eventually, after what was probably far too much deliberation, he decided on an approach. "Nice night for a swing, huh?"

The wind blew and the forest came alive with the sound of branches.

The girl didn't answer.

Thinking she was ignoring him, he began to feel a pressure building in him and briefly thought about simply getting in his car and driving away to escape it. He might have, but there was just something about this girl. He repeated the question, louder this time.

He was rewarded with an upward glance and a, "What?"

"A swing. A nice night for it, huh?"

"A what?" She was cupping one hand to her ear and motioning him forward with the other.

Arthur walked forward, then hesitated and backpedaled a step before continuing on. "Swinging, I said. A good night."

He was still some distance away, and the girl again couldn't quite make out what he was saying. "Oh. Goodnight to you, too." A little wave, and on she went swinging.

"No. Not 'goodnight'. It's a good night. For swinging." He was right up next to her, but his nervousness was so great that he couldn't even face her; he kept his face half-buried in the shoulder of his button-up shirt when she looked at him.

Her eyes were a cloudy shade of amber, glassy like an agate marble, with eyebrows much darker than her hair that formed the slightest bit of a unibrow. Arthur was never socially graceful, but he was usually better than this.

"Ahhh," she finally said. "I like swinging. It's fun."

"Yes, yes, very fun."

Arthur just stood as the girl swung. She was now knocking her feet together at the height of her swings. This sent a shower of dirt raining down with each clap. Arthur said the only thing he could think of.

"Your feet are really dirty." It was a stupid thing to say, and he immediately regretted it. As far as opening lines went, insulting the hygiene of a girl's feet had to be among the worst. He rubbed the thumb of his right hand against his palm, trying to recapture just a sliver of the peace and happiness he had felt earlier at Molly's. His hand felt wrinkled and old. Surely this beautiful, fun-loving creature would have no need of a man with such old, wrinkled hands. He turned to go, shuffling awkwardly back to the waiting Cougar. He was brought sharply back around by her cry of dismay.

"Oh no, you're right!" She had now stopped her swinging and sat with her legs fully extended, toes up, examining her feet with a look of fear on her face. "My daddy would be terribly upset with me. I'm always getting myself in the worst messes."

And just like that she burst into tears, hiding her face in her hands and sobbing hard enough that the swing once again began to move slightly back and forth.

Arthur was at a loss. What an odd girl.

He had a cousin, Sarah, who had a face like a moon pie and the mind of a child. Arthur had always liked Sarah, and the two got along great. In fact, when Sarah became angry one Thanksgiving and put her fist through a window out of frustration when they had unexpectedly run out of cranberry sauce at dinner, it was Arthur who sat with her on the couch and watched Snow White until she was calm enough that they could wrap her bloody hand with gauze. She was so distracted by his explanation of the dwarves and their various characteristics that she was practically tranquil. Arthur enjoyed talking to her, and he had been a little sad when the ambulance finally showed up to take Sarah to the hospital.

The swinging girl reminded him of his cousin. Something around the eyes, where everything didn't seem to quite lock into place. Except that where Sarah was a great, hulking ox of a girl, this pigtailed wisp was slender and beautiful. She didn't talk like Sarah either, whose voice was too slow and too long and too loud. Arthur couldn't image this one punching out a pane of glass over a blob of gelatinous fruit.

He walked back over and raised his hand to touch her shoulder, to comfort her as he had seen people in movies do, but stopped just short of lowering his hand. It seemed wrong somehow, invasive.

"Well," he finally said. "They aren't THAT dirty. I've seen dirtier." It was all he could think of to say.

"You have?" The girl brightened considerably at this.

"Oh, yeah. Much dirtier."

"Really?" She had stopped crying and was now wiping the wetness away from her cheeks. She was so beautiful. "You aren't just saying that?"

"No, not at all. I've seen feet twice as dirty. Three times as dirty."

The girl laughed.

Arthur wanted her to keep laughing, to keep liking him so he continued. "Ten times as dirty. I knew a girl whose feet were just little mud balls with toenail polish on them."

"You're silly."

Arthur's face dropped. He didn't want to be silly. He wanted to be charming.

Seeing his expression, she added, "I like silly."

Not knowing what else to do, he waited several seconds and then used his two index fingers to pull open his mouth so that he could stick out his tongue and make a funny face. Arthur felt like an imbecile, but the beautiful girl laughed again, a musical sound that mingled with the metallic jingle of the swing chains and the rattle of the branches in the breeze. Hearing that, he was content to be an imbecile for the rest of his life.

"I'm Rowan," she said, making a business-like expression and extending one rust-streaked hand.

When Arthur shook it, she couldn't maintain her seriousness any longer and exploded in amusement once more. He had no idea what was so funny, but he desperately wanted her to like him, so he laughed, too. "Arthur," he replied, once she had settled down.

"Arthur, Arthur, Arthur, Arthur. Aaaaaarrrrrthhhhhhhuuuuurrr. Ar-thur. Arth-ur." She said his name quickly, then slowed it down, spread it out. Tried it on like a new glove, stretched it in every way imaginable. After getting the shape of it, she said, "Arthur," and nodded as if accepting that it was, in fact, his name. Then, before he could say anything else, she added, "I'm hungry, Arthur. Do you like peanut butter and jelly?"

Arthur did like peanut butter and jelly and told her so. In response, she dipped back and shot forward a few times, rattling the chains and surprising Arthur with her aggressive swinging before suddenly springing into the air, only to come down an instant later in a mud puddle a few feet away. The impact of her landing coated her feet and sent brown water sloshing onto Arthur's Dockers. This would have normally displeased him—Arthur was a meticulous man—but he didn't have time to think on it. A second later, he was darting forward to steady Rowan as she seemed certain to lose her footing and fall back into the mud. His dress shoes were poorly suited to such a task, however, and he found himself slipping also. When he reached the girl, he succeeded only in sending them both tumbling to the muddy ground.

All her previous amusement had just been a prelude to the giggle she let out as they both sat, propped up on their hands, illuminated by headlights, in the cold muck of the puddle. Arthur tried to give her a stern look, but her grinning face, speckled with mud, was so honestly pleased and joyful that he couldn't manage to do it. Moments later, Arthur was laughing, too. This time, he got the joke.

They fell twice more—one fall, Arthur was fairly sure, Rowan caused on purpose—before, hands and arms entwined, they managed to use each other as fulcrums and stand up. His shirt was a mess and the backs of his thighs were soaked and chilly with puddle water. She pointed and laughed at his wet bottom and then turned around and asked if hers was similarly damp.

Being such a thin girl, her butt was modest but well-shaped and absolutely caked with mud. Arthur could barely make out under all of the filth the raised flower pattern on her back pockets that matched the design on the front. When he didn't immediately answer, Rowan flipped up her jacket and t-shirt to reveal the skin of her lower back and then looked over her shoulder with a questioning expression. "Well?"

Arthur felt his masculinity stir at the sight of her flesh, the smooth and supple curve of her back above the waistband of her jeans and the perfect sculpting of her mud-splattered, slender thighs stretching out from the legs of her shorts. And in between, the allure of her bottom.

Even without the blue magic, Arthur felt himself swell a little for the charming waif with the sleigh-bell laugh. He searched her eyes for any sign of seduction but found none. She was completely unaware of what she was doing to him.

"No," he said with a blush. "You're perfect."

She flashed him a wolf's grin and skipped over toward a pair of large stumps.

"Where are you going?" Arthur asked.

"To get lunch, silly."

"Lunch? It's after midnight."

"My daddy said lunch is any meal that keeps you from starving but leaves you wanting more. Don't matter what time it comes." She sat on one of the stumps, and then, reaching behind it, she produced a small Igloo cooler. She motioned to the other stump and called out to Arthur, "Aren't you eating?"

Arthur walked over, moving awkwardly with his wet pants and pausing to pull the fabric from between his butt cheeks. Sitting on the empty stump, he asked the girl, "Do your parents live around here? Do you? This is an odd place to swing. Why are you out here?"

She pressed the release button and slid open the cooler, revealing the silvered sheen of a Capri Sun, a sandwich in a baggie, a Snack Pack pudding, a butter knife, and a spoon. "Not far. And what's so odd about it? Why're you here, if it's so odd?"

There was a defensive edge to her voice, and Arthur worried that he had offended her. "I wasn't saying..." He trailed off and said nothing more while she retrieved the baggie and swooshed it around in her hands. She undid the Ziploc and tore the PB&J as evenly as she could. She wasn't particularly successful, and the whole process ended up being fairly messy. When she extended a smushed and ripped-up bit of sandwich toward Arthur, peanut butter clung to her index finger and jelly leaked down her wrist.

Arthur looked down at his filthy hands and then back at the sandwich half. Rowan gave him an exasperated look. Not wishing to further offend, he hastily wiped what muck he could off on his pants and took the offering. She didn't immediately take a bite of her half, and he realized that she was waiting for him as if he were a guest. He chanced a nibble and found the bread somewhat soggy and the peanut butter of less-than-stellar quality. Lying, he said, "Yum," and nodded a thank you toward her. Still, she did not eat.

Arthur waited, sure he had done something wrong. Eventually, she said, "I don't like the crust." Arthur waited again. He nodded blankly. Rowan raised her eyebrows.

"Oh?" Arthur smacked his lips and looked at her curiously. "Oh!" He finally figured it out. Setting his sandwich on his knee, he reached into the cooler and picked out the butter knife. Moving slowly, still uncertain if he was getting it right, he took her half from her and, placing it on his other knee, did his best to cut off the crust with the knife. It was sloppy work in the indirect light of the Mercury's headlights, and his knee was a less-than-ideal surface, but he managed to separate the crust and hand her back a trimmed piece. By this point, the scrap of sandwich, between the tearing and the cutting, was just a clump of bread and goo, but Rowan smiled with pleasure when she took a bite. She chewed loudly and with relish, and when she spoke, Arthur could see food in her mouth.

"Thank you. My daddy used to do that for me."

"My mother, too," said Arthur.

"Is your mother living?"

"No." Arthur frowned at this. He had been what some people called a Mama's Boy, sleeping in the same bed as his mother up until he was twelve. Even then, he cried when she forced him to sleep in his own, by-then-too-small sailboat bed with its nautical designs and lighthouse covers. It was his erections that ruined it. His mother hated his erections. Arthur grew to hate them, too. He still did. Maybe that's why they rarely came around anymore without assistance.

"Mine neither. What happened to your mom?" A spurt of raspberry jam oozed out onto her cheek, and she tilted her head this way and that trying to get it to drip back into her mouth. Arthur wanted to help, to use his finger to scoop up the sugary spread and place it on her tongue, but he resisted the urge. She would have been powerfully offended by such an act. And if she wasn't, he would be.

"Stroke." Arthur answered as if it had been only the one, but that wasn't the truth.

The first one had set her to pouring orange juice on her cereal and eating it with a fork. She averaged one every couple of months for two years after that. Her eleventh had reduced her to singing the alphabet out of rhythm and rarely finishing the whole song. Arthur, who had moved her into his house by the dump at that point despite recommendations from the doctors, would spend his evenings after work when he didn't have a date singing with her and then carrying her to his bed at the conclusion of the night.

By day, she sat in the green chair by the window and sang and shit herself while the television blared until one day she got to "T" and no further. He still carried her into his bed for days after. He lay next to her as her body stiffened, then grew supple once more. Arthur stayed stiff the entire time. No magic needed. "Yours?"

"They both died in an accident. You remind me of my daddy a

little. You got the same hair."

Arthur touched the remnants of his hair. Just the slightest pressure yielded the feel of his scalp. He'd gone gray early, in his thirties, and turned toward snow before his season. He had little more than white fuzz at this point. He was a dandelion in a muddy dress shirt.

Digging into the cooler, Rowan grabbed the Capri Sun. After tearing the plastic wrapping off with her teeth, she twirled the pointed straw in her fingers and made a show of stabbing at the silver pouch. No matter the force of her attempt, the curve of the container seemed to deflect her attacks. If she hadn't looked so earnest, her tongue hanging out one side of her pretty mouth in concentration, Arthur might have laughed. She still had jam on her face. If she focused much harder, she might taste it.

After watching her struggle for about a half a minute, he stuffed the remainder of his sandwich in his mouth and held his hands out for the pouch, his eyes questioning above his bulging cheeks.

She smiled broadly, revealing a raspberry seed stuck between her two front teeth, before shoving the drink into his hands. When he speared the entry hole with a single, well-placed thrust, she clapped her hands together rapidly and said, "Goody, goody, goody."

Having never heard a real-live person say the phrase, Arthur found himself even more smitten. He handed her the pouch and gave her his best smile, which wasn't all that great as far as smiles went. Crinkling the pouch, she sucked so hard that she went fish-faced when she took her first drink, and his smile grew large enough to hurt his face.

"Mmmmm! Very Berry, my favorite!"

With the Capri Sun more than half-gone after the first drink, she extended it back to Arthur. He took a sip while she held it in her outstretched hand. When he couldn't get at the liquid and produced only slurping noises, she gave it a squeeze and shot a burst of sweetened liquid into his mouth, surprising him and causing him to gush fluid out of his nose and cough violently. It burned his nasal passages and tasted like chemicals and flavored ChapStick.

"Good, huh?" she asked without a hint of sarcasm. Arthur could only manage a strangled noise and a thumbs-up. He would have guzzled a gallon of Very Berry to spend another second in the light of her smile.

Arthur was very much in love by this point. Like he had been with Molly earlier in the evening.

Except that Rowan was different. He was certain of it. Still, he had to be sure. Unable to help himself, he just blurted it out.

"Rowan, do you know what a blowjob is?"

The young girl in the little girl outfit turned a deep shade of scarlet. When she nodded, Arthur's heart sank. "Uh-huh, but proper girls aren't supposed to do it. Do you want me to show you?"

The older man's eyes went sad, and he nodded. Somewhere in the back of his mind, the two wolf heads on his black bag slid past each other with a click.

"Well, do you?" She seemed nervous and embarrassed. At least she had that decency, Arthur thought. He couldn't bear to vocalize his disappointment, so he nodded, already thinking about how he was going to grab her wrists together and force her to the ground. At least the dump was just through the woods. He'd have to ready another barrel. No rest for the righteous.

She locked eyes with him, all seriousness. For the first time, she seemed her actual age, an adult. She was almost sultry. It was awful. Then she leaned forward with exaggerated slowness, her lips opening, her tongue darting out.

Arthur hated her now. Hated her worse than all of the others combined. She was the trickiest yet. Only the thought of how bright her soul might glow if properly extracted kept him from grabbing her by the hair and smashing her brains out on the stump.

Bent forward, she looked up at him, her face between his chin and his lap. She gave a shy smile. "I can't do it with you looking. Close your eyes," she said.

He did and began counting down from five. He would have to stun her. One blow to the side of the temple should do it, small girl like her. Then he could get his tools and—

The sound was almost deafening. His eyes shot open, and he saw her inches from his face, Capri Sun and straw held to his left ear, just blowing with everything she had. The pouch was expanded near to the point of bursting. With a quick inhale, she brought it back to a crumple. Then she puffed out again. Each time it made the same rude noise. She did it for the better part of a minute, playing it like an instrument while Arthur looked on incredulously.

Rowan only stopped when she grew lightheaded. Arthur felt a little lightheaded himself.

After she was done, she did her best to hide her giggles and look contrite. "I'm sorry. I know that's not proper manners for a young lady. Daddy used to yell at me for doing it at the table."

"A blowjob. A blowjob?" Arthur nodded the admission out of her. When she gave a guilty acknowledgment, he started to giggle, too. "A blowjob. THAT was a blowjob?"

"Yep."

Arthur stared. She stuck her tongue at him. It was purple. He returned the gesture. She let him know that his was as well. They both giggled until Arthur feared he might urinate.

She was the funniest, most perfect girl in the entire world, he decided. He was going to marry her, and they were going to have a dozen babies. And she was going to be the best mother ever. Arthur was sure of it.

The wind picked up again, running through the trees and causing as much racket as a set of cans tied to a limousine. Too much racket, actually. Arthur looked up and noticed them for the first time.

It wasn't only branches that were rattling, as he thought earlier, but wind chimes, dozens of them, hanging from boughs and small limbs alike. Many of them looked quite intricate, pale wood with the bark shaved off, though Arthur could see little detail that high up, out of the beams of his headlights. They clattered like drumsticks to a rhythmic beat, speeding up with the wind until they were as loud and long as a screech owl. Arthur waited until it was quiet enough to speak and then asked, "How'd those get up there?"

Rowan turned shy again, averting her eyes. After dropping the shriveled Capri Sun into the cooler, she lifted out the pudding and the spoon.

"You?" Arthur was incredulous.

She nodded and used the tip of her tongue to try to leverage up the foil that covered the top of the Snack Pack.

Arthur looked up again, noting the height. Some of them were hung what must have been a hundred feet up. He watched the girl as she put the raised edge of the metallic cover in her mouth and tore it open with one quick motion. "Wow," was all he could say.

Rowan turned the foil around and licked the sweetness that clung to its underside. "I'm a real good climber. Just like Jack Spriggins with his enchanted bean."

Arthur's heart grew two sizes, and it still wasn't enough to contain the swell of love that he experienced. "You like fairy tales?" He asked the question so quickly and with such excitement that the syllables threatened to run past each other and turn his words to gibberish.

"What's a fairy tale?" Rowan extended a spoonful of pudding toward Arthur's mouth. He brushed it away, too excited by the turn in the conversation.

"A fairy tale. A fable. You know, a legend?"

She gave a suit-yourself shrug of her shoulders and ate the spoonful of pudding. "Old-timeys? Marchens?"

Arthur gave her a blank look.

In response, Rowan drew herself up, spine straight, and made as severe of an expression as her little girl face would allow. "Fee-fi-fo-fum! I smell the blood of a Puritan. Be he alive, or be he dead, I'll grind his bones to make my bread." Then she plunged her spoon into the pudding and took an oversized bite, looking as fierce as she could manage, before she laughed at her own joke, mouth wide, tapioca balls stuck to her tongue like pearls in a clam.

She'd gotten the first part wrong, but Arthur didn't care. Here she was. He'd waited so long.

"Yes." Finally. His princess. "Do you know many?"

Arthur knew most of them. From obscure ones such as The Boy Who Drew Cats and Corvetto, to the well-known classics like Rapunzel and The Billy Goats Gruff.

Rowan gave a sheepish look. "Pretty many. Even though daddy didn't like 'em none."

"He didn't like them?" Arthur couldn't imagine such a stupid man.

"He said they were a bad influence."

Arthur scoffed. "A bad influence? How?" He took exception to even the implication that such stories could be bad. An image of his mother reading to him when he was a child snuggled into his mind. Arthur was curled into the crook of her arm, a Tiffany lamp casting a rainbow of light across the pages, her breast pressing firmly against his cheek, separated only by the thin cotton of her nightgown. The Big Bad Wolf huffing and puffing the scent of her Oil of Olay moisturizing cream into his nostrils.

"Well," Rowan said, looking just on the verge of shame. "My Granny was the one who would tell 'em to me."

"Why was that bad?"

There was real sadness in her eyes when she answered. Regret even. "She was like me. Touched."

Arthur looked into Rowan's big eyes. They were so round, empty of guilt, empty of guile, he felt like he might fall in. Even then, there would have been plenty of room. Touched in the head. "You mean... special?" He imagined the grandmother reading in his cousin Sarah's mongoloid voice.

The girl winced at the word. She had sense enough for that. Arthur regretted saying it. "Yeah. Special."

"Well," Arthur began, searching for the right thing to say. He was so bad at this. Just once he wanted the words to come easy like they did to him when he was working on skin. "You are special. Special special. Not special...you know."

She brightened a little but seemed unconvinced. "You really think? Even if I'm...touched?"

"I know... I've known a lot of people. A lot of women." Arthur made a face. "Well, not like that. I don't mean like that."

"Like what?" Rowan seemed to be honestly asking.

"Never mind," Arthur answered uncomfortably. "The point is, most women are ugly. Ugly inside. Monsters. You're...something different." The word came to him. "You're a princess."

"That's what Granny used to say." Rowan showed all of her teeth. Her smile was huge.

"Smart lady." It slipped out of him before he thought better of it. He hoped the young girl didn't overthink it.

She didn't. She never overthought anything. She just grinned and then grinned some more, then interspersed her grins with big bites of pudding. When she was down to the last bit, she scooped it off the sides of the plastic container and held it out once more toward her guest.

Arthur refused her pudding advances and asked her the same question he asked every woman he dated, the same question he asked himself every day. "What fairy tale character would you be?"

This time, she refused to answer him until he took the bite. Moving the spoon in an erratic flight pattern, she brought it to his lips while making airplane noises. The wind shook the wind chimes, and he and Rowan had a dogfight over dessert. The third time she pressed the coolness of the pudding to his lips, he begrudgingly swallowed it.

"Well?" he blurted before it was even all the way down his throat.

She pointed at him and pantomimed a disgusted face. "Ewww, you just ate birds' eyes. Ewwwwwww!"

Impatiently, Arthur grabbed her hands and held them tight. They were larger than he would have guessed, almost as long as his own, with dirty nails that she dug into his palms out of surprise. "Tell me," he said more urgently than he intended. "Just think about it."

Most girls picked one of the famous ones from the Disney movies.

Not Rowan.

She looked at him apprehensively. "I don't have to think. I know. Granny used to tell me."

"Which story?"

"My story."

"Your story?"

"Yes."

"Tell me."

"Granny told it better. She'd always tell it the same way. We'd sit in our special chairs, and she'd say to me, 'Rowan Griswold, did you hear it tell that you're a princess, nice and true?' And I'd say, 'No, Granny Griswold, I ain't never.' Even though, really, I had."

"Was she your mother's mother, then?" Arthur asked.

"Kind of. I called her Granny. She had a couple 'greats' in there, but she always told me she was an old woman with precious little time left and not given the luxury to suffer fools or formalities, so she had me call her Granny. She told a mighty story. Since she ain't here, I'll tell it best I can."

"You'll do great," Arthur said.

"I ain't so sure. When she was talking, I'd prompt her, as I was taught. She always liked me to ask her things, like she was calling out and I was answering. It took me a long time because Granny was hard to figure with her accent and I wasn't very quick to learn. But I ain't never told no Marchens to nobody before."

"Well, how did you prompt her?"

"I'd say, 'If I's a princess, how came I to be here?' That's how she talked. And when I was with her, I talked the same."

"What did she say?"

"She'd answer, 'Ain't no path too narrow under the light of the bright moon.'"

"Was she from the South?" Arthur asked.

"Back East," Rowan replied.

"Where back East? Connecticut?"

"Don't think so."

"You don't know?"

"Granny always said the same thing, 'We're from the old lands, from a time when the Rhine river was still Rain, the Griswolds was still Stumps, before there was white in my hair, or would have been yellow in yours, little Rowan. We were pureblood then. German. Tall and gray as the trees in that country, before my son Peter, your daddy's granddaddy, picked a poppy and brought that ruddy Irish blood to your cheeks and honey to your head. You's a mutt, but a cute one, and I love you fine, even if you's cursed as an owl at noon. 'Course, so am I,' she'd say."

"Cursed?" Arthur asked.

"I'll get to that." Rowan shot Arthur an irritated glance. "Granny said all stories was true. Every last one." Rowan fell into a singsong rhythm that said she'd heard this said the same way many times before and learned it by heart. 'She'd seen a bee sting anyone that came too close to the orange tree that it was in love with. Seen a girl dressed for a ball by doves and chosen as a queen for the way her foot smushed into a pair of squirrel fur slippers. Seen a goose the color of spun gold that caused laughing madness in anyone who slept on a pillow stuffed with its feathers.

"All true?" Arthur believed in fairy tales, but not even he believed that much.

"To hear her tell it, each word in those old Marchens was gospel. Trouble was, everybody had the wrong hymn books. The stories people knew were just enough wrong that they didn't see the truth of them when they gawked at it. More, the stories was always repeating. People just stumbled in and got tangled up in old yarns willy-nilly. Never even noticed for the most part, because it wasn't exactly the old-timey they knew."

"What does this have to do with you?"

"Cause, Granny said I was one of the stumblers. Wasn't my fault for being the way I was or her being the same. We was both caught up in our stories."

Arthur was fascinated, but he was becoming frustrated with the runaround. "And what was your story?"

She sang on in the way she'd learned. "In the old country, there was a place called Old Rinkrank by some. It was a mountain of glass, tall and shiny in the sun. Even had a village built under it. Some called it Glasberg, though Granny said the people living there now call it something else, and they done cleaned all the glass off so it's just dirt and rock and boring stuff now."

Arthur looked over his shoulder at the dump and then raised an eyebrow at the girl.

"Granny said a handful of bad pennies like my family, with our history, couldn't help but settle here, under our own glass mountain. Strange calls to strange. Mama and daddy did what mamas and daddies do, and I was born ill-fated as a stopped clock."

"How were you ill-fated? You mean because you're…?"

"Yep."

"Honey…" Arthur wasn't accustomed to feeling pity, but he felt it heavy in his breast listening to this sweet girl. "That's genetics and environmental factors. It's science. Not a curse."

She looked sad again for a second. "Daddy said that. Thought maybe they could fix me. Wanted to take me to special doctors. Granny said I didn't need to be fixed. I ain't very smart, but whether it's science or a curse don't make it no more fair."

Arthur felt so guilty that he didn't interrupt her again.

"In the old world, in the shadow of the glass mountain was a castle. Locked inside the castle lived a cursed princess. Some will say enchanted, but it weren't so. It was cursed. On the mountain were apple trees, taller than any apple tree had a right to be, only instead of apples, they grew keys of ivory, each a different shape. Only one would fit the lock in the castle so that the princess could be set free.

"Many knights tried and failed to conquer the slickness of the mountain, and their armor littered the mountain. Metal on glass. Shine on shine.

"One knight made it halfway, but when he went for the top, he was attacked by the magical eagles that guarded the keys.

"Eventually, a prince happened along. He killed a mountain lion and used its claws to climb. Even still, he grew tired and rested on the slope. Sensing he was easy pickin's, the eagles attacked. But the prince grabbed onto them and they, in trying to shake free, carried him to the top, where he found the right key and entered the castle and saved the princess, breaking the curse."

Arthur had heard the story before, even if the details were slightly different. His mother had done the same thing, adjusting the tales to suit him. For a significant portion of his childhood, he actually thought he was King Arthur. He pictured a step-slow grandma doing the same for a big-eyed Rowan.

They were meant for each other. And if she were his princess…

"So," she asked bashfully. "I've been wondering… Are you a prince? Did you come here to save me?"

She waited on his answer like a girl leaning out of a tower window. It was so clear now, who he was, what he was.

"Yes," he answered with no reservations.

Her saucer eyes were all excitement. "I knew it! My Granny said I'd know my prince because he would love me for the real me. He'd be a gentleman and a knight and he'd watch over me when she was gone."

Most women grew uglier as he talked to them. Not so with Rowan. He looked at her full-on, with her thick eyebrows and jam-stained face. She was beautiful. He said the thing she most wanted to hear in the entire world. "Take me to your castle, my princess."

She nodded enthusiastically, then a concerned look crossed her face and she looked up. "Okay, but shouldn't you find the right key?"

Arthur craned his neck up at the wind chimes and tried to determine how many seconds it would take for him to fall from the top of the canopy to the ground. "That's okay. I don't need it." Rowan eyed him skeptically. "Would your prince lie to you?"

Rowan turned the question over in her mind like a car with a broken timing belt. Her mind cranked and cranked but never got anywhere. Fingers still entwined with hers, he freed his thumb and used it to gently stroke the back of her hand. This seemed to calm her concerns where logic had failed.

They stood together, leaving the cooler where it lay, and holding hands, Rowan led Arthur in the direction of the school. A few steps in and she changed to skipping. She urged her prince to do the same. He initially refused, but her youthful energy was infectious. By the time they reached the rusted side entrance of the school, the man the newspapers had once dubbed "The Grimm Reaper" was skipping as well, on knees that creaked like a dungeon door.

Neither thought to leave bread crumbs.

Chapter Four

If laughter had ever filled the halls of the old school, it had peeled away with the paint on the walls. The outside had long ago found the inside, and the only sound that echoed as Arthur and Rowan made their way was the crunch of twigs under their feet and the cheerful mumble of the girl humming "Ring Around the Rosie."

The place was pungent with the smell of animal urine, and Arthur noticed raccoon droppings piled in the corners. Only a scattering of too-small desks in the rooms they passed, and a few surviving-but-faded handprints in various colors that were on the parts of the walls gave any indication that this had once been a place for children.

It was hard to imagine anyone living here. It was the house from The Old Woman Who Lived in The Shoe foreclosed on by the bank and rented out by ghosts.

"You live here?" Arthur asked.

"Yep. Granny, too, before she passed."

"Your parents?"

"No. They lived in a house not far from here. They didn't come here unless they had to. Once a month or so. Granny took care of me most of the time."

A mentally challenged girl left in the care of her mentally challenged grandmother in the husk of a ruined school. Arthur wished he could have met Rowan's parents. Told them a story. Told a story with them.

She led the older man to a room unlike any of the others. There was no stink of urine, only the pungent scent of a kerosene lamp that sat on what was once a teacher's desk and filled the room with flickering light. The floors had been cleaned of debris and feces. In the middle of the room was a collection of tables that had been pushed together to make one big round one. Stacked high on the big table were crayons of every imaginable color, scissors, bottles of paste at various levels of fullness. And plastered on the walls, affixed with copious amounts of Scotch Tape, were pictures of princes. There was Charming and Phillip, Prince Eric, Prince Adam, Aladdin, even the frog prince with his green skin.

Rowan had been waiting for him just as Arthur had been waiting for her.

She smiled and detached herself from him without a word. Sitting at the table, she gathered an assortment of crayons and, using one arm to shield her project from his view, began to scribble profusely on a blank piece of lined paper.

Arthur was content to just watch her at first. The light of the lamp seemed to cling to her, almost like she was glowing.

Arthur opened the compartment on his keychain and shook out a blue pill into his hand, and then another just to be sure. They caught on the nervous lump in his throat and turned sour in his mouth. Tonight was the night.

After he had choked them down, he sat near her at the big table and began working on his own project. When she tried to peek, he admonished her and piled the unused supplies so that they created a fort around him to protect his privacy. Rowan giggled.

They worked like that for about fifteen minutes. The Viagra was giving him a headache, and his vision had tinted blue by the time they were both through, but he hardly noticed. Arthur couldn't remember being happier.

She held up her coloring. It was a picture of her—Arthur could tell because of the pigtails—inside of a cage. A depiction of Arthur, dressed in white and with a frosting of pale hair, stood some distance away holding up a funny looking key. Rays of sunlight shot forth from it.

Arthur took the piece of art from her, folded it up, and placed it in the left-hand pocket of his shirt. Then he made a show of patting it and rubbing it against his chest where his heart was. Rowan seemed pleased.

She seemed downright giddy when he showed her what he had made. It was a tiara of yellow construction paper, held together at the back by tape and a smear of paste. The points weren't even, and the little gems he'd drawn on the front looked more like cherries than precious stones, but when he placed it on her head, she squealed with delight.

Then Arthur did something he never did; he made the first move.

He kissed her. It was sloppy, and she still tasted like pudding, but it was pure in every other respect.

It was the best kiss of his life. It was the first kiss that didn't make him sick.

His pharmacy-grade hardness stretched his pants. He reached for her.

"No 'ever after' yet," she said. "You have to climb into my room and rescue me first."

"Isn't this your room?" He was confused.

"My bedroom, silly. This is my playroom."

Arthur's need for her, for her glow, spurred him forward. They stood, left the room, and walked down the hall, with Rowan leading the way, her tiara bobbing on her head, Arthur bobbing after it.

She led him to an old iron door. It was rusted, and the ground was covered in brown flakes from the opening and closing of it. A sign still affixed to it read, in barely legible letters, "Keep Out: Maintenance."

It took all of Rowan's strength to open it.

It was the boiler room.

Pipes that had once carried water to sinks and heat to classrooms crisscrossed the space. The entire area still smelled like grease and oil, though it had probably been some time since it had seen either. Wood smoke was heavy on the air, and Arthur could see light bouncing off the walls of an elevated section on the other side of the room. Must be a wood-burning stove or fireplace. It was noticeably hotter here than in the rest of the school, and the warmth had evidently attracted wildlife seeking a snug place to winter, as the animal stench was stronger here than anywhere.

It was hard for Arthur to see, but Rowan navigated the maze of valves and pipes by memory. She led him by the hand to the ladder, where she climbed up and he followed.

The smoke smell was coming from a furnace, into which a collection of logs had been stuck. The flames inside had begun to fade. Rowan fixed this by adding a log from a stacked pile and then prodding the wood with a pipe that leaned against the furnace. The fire huffed sparks and ash in annoyance at being awakened so abruptly, but after a few pokes, it was dancing energetically once more.

The room came into focus under its illuminating limbs.

The only thing that made it a "bedroom" was an old, worn mattress shoved into one corner. Even in the dim light, it looked shabby and soiled, and its stink threatened to overpower the smell of the burning wood. The only blanket was the tattered remains of a neon orange hunting coat.

A table stood to one side. On it were pots of all sizes. Arthur could see bits of old food stuck to the lips and sides of most of them. A shelf filled with books sat as far away from the fire as was possible.

Two chairs faced each other in front of the furnace, one large, one small. They were bolted to the floor, and the arms sported shackles, the locks of which were broken.

Arthur was dumbfounded.

"The chairs?"

"Granny's and mine." Her voice was sad.

"They locked you up. Your parents. The both of you. For being special? What kind of people would..."

"They said they had to. It was for our own good."

"You poor thing." Arthur walked to the bookshelf and pulled a thick, leather-bound tome off it. It was heavy in his hands. The pages were wavy and brown with age, stiff against his fingers. He opened it. On left-hand pages, in flowing script, were sentences in a language he didn't understand. The pages on the right had the story in English. He began reading.

"What will you give me if I spin the straw this time?"

"I have nothing more that I could give you," answered the girl.

The odd little man pointed to the swollen belly of the miller's daughter where her child grew.

The girl nodded. "Should I fetch a blade?"

"We will have no need of metal this night."

The man sat her in the chair next to the spinning wheel and reel. He lifted her dress until it bunched on her hips and her thighs were bare before him. He pressed his fingers together like he was diving into a lake and forged into her. The miller's daughter began lamenting and crying, but the man took no pity on her.

He twisted this way and that. Her womanhood grew slick despite her fear. The burden in her belly grew heavier still, and so did her pleasure. The little man pulled both from her with his hands.

"Say my name. Say my name and give me what is mine."

The cries of new life echoed off the stone walls of the spinning room, and above even that, the woman's cries of pleasure.

"Rumpelstiltskin! Rumpelstiltskin!"

Rumplestiltskin? That wasn't right, thought Arthur.

He turned back toward Rowan and found her sitting in the smaller chair wearing an anxious expression. "Rowan," he asked. "Who wrote this?"

"Granny." Why did she seem so nervous. Was she sweating?

Arthur glanced back at the elegant handwriting in two languages. "But your grandmother was slow."

Rowan snorted. "Granny was the smartest person I ever met."

"You said she was like you, touched in the head ."

Rowan looked right at him. "She was. Cursed. And it's not just the head; it's all of me."

"Cursed?" Something was wrong. This wasn't the right story. None of these were the right stories.

"Cursed." Rowan suddenly cried out in pain. Something moved beneath her skin. In the poor lighting, Arthur could have sworn it was her bones. "We have to hurry up," she said.

The young girl's face was a mask of worry and swaying shadows.

"Rowan, those are just stories. They're not re—"

The little finger on her right hand bent over itself and snapped back against the side of her hand. She screamed. "Use the key!"

Arthur looked at her. Really looked at her. He noticed her eyes, her teeth, remembered the feel of her hands in his own.

Arthur Rosenbaum was a calm man. He reminded himself of that several times. When he almost had himself convinced, he asked her another question. "What happened to your grandmother, Rowan?"

Her voice sounded weird when she answered, as if it were coming from down deep in her chest. Too deep. Deeper than a little girl should have gone. Deeper than anyone human should go. "A hunter found her sleeping in the woods and cut her open. He fi—"

"Filled her belly with stones and sank her in the river." Arthur's voice sounded hollow in his ears. He glanced at the orange coat. "Your parents, what time of month did they come? What happened to them? What kind of accident was it?"

Rowan didn't answer except to let out another yell. No, not a yell. A howl. She was trembling. Her body seemed heavier and longer now. The chair was shaking from the force of her shuddering. The unlocked shackles jangled and flapped against the wood of the armrests. Her paper tiara tumbled to the ground, knocked off by her new ears. The thing that wasn't quite Rowan said in a voice that wasn't quite Rowan's, "Use the key, my prince."

Only Arthur didn't have any key. Because he wasn't a prince. This wasn't a story about princes.

Arthur knew what character he was now.

He ran. Back toward the road, back toward the path he never should have left.

Chapter Five

The school was dark, and without Rowan to lead him, Arthur stumbled and fell, banged his head on a pipe before he even made it out of the boiler room, stubbed his still-erect dick on the door. He slipped in a pile of shit outside of the cafeteria and took a fall that swelled his wrist almost immediately. But he didn't dare stop.

He could hear her. He could smell her. Her scent was everywhere. It always had been.

He hit the double doors that opened to the playground as if he were shot from a gun. With legs that burned from age and exertion, he went full-bore toward his Cougar.

When he reached it, he stopped in his tracks.

Crows. They cocked their heads at him and cried their warning There must have been a hundred of them, so thick on his car that he could barely see a patch of beige beneath the black of their feathers and the white of their excrement.

The soldiers had come out to guard the exit.

Arthur made for the door, and they came at him as a murder, swarming and pecking, driving him back with their talons and cawing laughter.

They took his will and a piece of his right ear. He hoped they'd simply carry him away, like in Rowan's story, but they showed him no such mercy.

The howling finally reached the open air of the outside.

Arthur had nowhere to go but up. He ran through the woods, lungs aching and blood rushing in his ears, toward the dump. Sure he'd never make it, he was shocked when he hit the slopes of trash.

Arthur tried to climb, but the mountain moved beneath him. No matter how vigorously he pumped his legs, he made only minimal progress. When he was barely a tenth of the way up, he came down hard on a piece of rebar. It pierced his calf and stuck out the other side.

Arthur screamed and fell and made it no further up the mountain.

Rowan emerged from the woods. A hirsute shape moving against the night, dark on dark. Only her eyes were the same, that unique amber color.

The mountain offered her no challenge, and she bounded up the sides on her thick, haunched legs. Arthur scooted on his butt like a crab, trying to scuttle up the side of the dump. All it earned him was a bottle cap-shaped tear in his palm.

When she stood right in front of him, backlit by the full of the moon, the thought occurred to him that she looked nothing like the stories said she did.

The muzzle wasn't as long, for one thing. And the face had none of a wolf's elegance. It was all teeth and stretched skin and spittle dripping from her chin.

She was tall, impossibly tall, and the joints of her arms and legs bent the wrong way. Still skinny, and not as hairy as he would have expected. Her ribs showed to the sides of a row of nipples caught somewhere between human and canine. Claws, long and twisted, jutted from knobby fingers and wide, padded feet.

There was an energy about her, a heat, some dark magic buried under her chest. It glowed like flame through her skin. It was hideous.

Caught without even a straw house, Arthur waited for the Big Bad Wolf to devour him.

But she didn't.

She tried to speak, but it was too garbled to comprehend.

She slid one clawed finger to the top of his neck. With a swipe down his torso, she tore the buttons from his dress shirt and exposed his chest. Another pass cleaved through the leather of his belt.

She tried again to speak with her wolf mouth. This time Arthur understood. Just one word.

Prince.

The she-wolf lowered herself halfway onto him. With horror, Arthur looked into her inhuman eyes. For once, even Arthur couldn't tell if there was guilt. She came the rest of the way down. Her skin was hot to the touch. Arthur Rosenbaum flopped like a fish under her full weight.

Rowan gave herself to her prince on the side of the glass mountain, animal lust mixing with plain old loneliness. Her hands tore into him. Blood ran from his wounds, soaked into his shirt and stained the picture folded in his pocket until even the white parts on the drawing of him were stained red.

Somewhere under all the glass, a dozen princes rolled over in their sleep and dreamed no more of unpleasant things.

Chapter Six

By five in the morning, the battery on the Mercury was almost dead. The headlights had weakened to the point that they barely illuminated the girl on the swing, or what she held in her hand. She had the red hood of her windbreaker pulled up now.

Most people didn't know this about Rowan, but she was a sculptor. Only she didn't like working with wood or clay.

She ran the edge of her pocket knife over the bones in her hands until they were smooth. Pressing firmly, she dug away at the points, made notches and canals, until they resembled the ends of keys. When she had several just right, she bound them together with a length of white hair. This chime wouldn't be too long. Not much to work with.

When the sun came up and she could see, she'd hang this one with the rest.

She couldn't remember what happened when she changed. Sometimes at first, she would have a terrible feeling, and she would want to run and find someone and scream at them and cry. But it was like a dark dream that faded with each step. The woods were large, and by the time she stumbled across someone, she could never remember what the nightmare had been about.

She knew the results, however. The wind chime gave a clatter when she shook it.

"Arthur," she said his name again. It was such a good name. A king's name.

She had been so sure this time. But he had been another false prince. A liar, just like the rest.

Only a real prince could save her.

Another would come. A better one, who would cut the crust off of her sandwiches without being reminded.

She liked the tiara, though. That had been nice.

Maybe the next would bring her a real one! A real prince with a real tiara!

Rowan liked that idea very much. It was romantic.

Rowan Griswold was quite a romantic.

The lights on the Mercury Cougar flicked off for good.

GRAVE MARKER

ROB SMALES

RED BLOOD, WHITE WOOD

DEDICATION

To anyone who's ever been in a nice thick fog and felt for a moment they might not be alone.

You weren't.

And for my father, Tom, who was a carpenter,
and my son, Tom, who is not.

Chapter One

"Stand to that door, Smythe, and let no one through barring emergency. Understood?"

"Aye, sir."

"Good man. Dismissed."

Yeoman Smythe chopped off a salute and stepped into the passageway, closing the cabin door with a *thud.* Admiral Buchanan barely registered the sound as, glancing at the thick, oilskin-wrapped packet on his desk, he strode to the porthole and peered out. Beside the *HMS Lionheart*, slightly distorted by imperfections in the thick glass, lay the *HMS Imperious.*

"The ghost ship," the admiral murmured, secure in the knowledge that no one could overhear.

They'd received word from the HMS *Imperius* that she was on the trail of a privateer, and come to meet her at Nassau. Captain Danforth was a punctual man—hard, in His Majesty's navy, to *not* be—and when the *Imperious* had been not one week late, but two, Admiral Buchanan had readied the *Lionheart* and set sail for her last known coordinates, hoping she'd not somehow run into more than she could handle.

This morning, the ninth into the voyage, the crow had called "Ship ahoy;" the *Imperious*, sails furled and adrift, floated towards the Bahamas in the current usually taken advantage of by merchants. Hailing had no effect as the *Lionheart* had drawn alongside, and there had been no motion on deck as grapnels had been employed to bind the ships together. Even as they'd been hailing, Buchanan had examined the *Imperious* through a glass and could find no hint of her crew.

First Mate Watchfield had led the boarding party and reported no sign of life. There were the marks of habitation, to be sure; clothes and other belongings belowdeck, stations where the workings of running a ship had been left half-finished—even food laid out in the galley, left untouched and rotting a-table. Two of the ship's launch boats were missing, but that wasn't nearly enough to attend to the *Imperious*'s crew of four hundred twenty-two. The men of the *Lionheart* had begun referring to it as *the ghost ship* almost immediately, and though the admiral had his officers quashing the appellation whenever they heard it, he had to admit—if only to himself—he found it fitting.

Buchanan turned from the porthole with a shudder. Before receiving Watchfield's report, he'd rather publicly stated his intention to board the *Imperious* himself in the morning; he couldn't change his mind now without lending credence to the whisperings of his superstitious crew.

He sat behind his desk and stared at the packet before him: an official document pouch of His Majesty's Navy found on Captain Danforth's desk and addressed to Buchanan himself. *Danforth's last report,* the admiral thought. *Sealed and awaiting a dispatch vessel when whatever happened… happened.* He poked the bundle, feeling the solidity, the weight of the thing. *Far too thick for a simple report, even this close to the colonies. Perhaps Danforth left some word as to why his entire crew might abandon ship, seemingly in the middle of a meal?*

Slitting the wax seal, he pulled out a great wad of paper, folded in thrice. He spread the document flat with a palm, and by the sunlight pouring through the porthole, began to read.

Chapter Two

August 14, 1743

To: Admiral Archibald Buchanan, HMS Lionheart

Re: Prisoner Timothy Carpenter, pirate (accused)

Admiral,

In a previous missive, I outlined the taking into custody of one Timothy Carpenter, crewman of the pirate ship Ravager under Captain Reginald Torvald. Carpenter is being held, and we continue our search for the Ravager, returning to the site of our confrontation with said privateer northwest of the Bahama Archipelago and using the prisoner's description of their flight to aid in its location. Carpenter's mere presence speaks to the imminence of our success. If we fail to locate the Ravager within the month, I will set sail for Nassau to rendezvous with the prison ship HMS Enclave, as previously outlined, and transfer the prisoner for sentencing and transportation.

The following is a transcript (prisoner Carpenter claims illiteracy) of what I believe to be a full and frank confession of his recent actions as a privateer and criminal. Though some of his tale appears the fanciful ramblings of a diseased mind, he otherwise appears quite sane, and I see none of the usual signs of "chasing the dragon," or any other such abuses men of his ilk are prone to.

—Hobart Danforth, Captain, HMS Imperious

Chapter Three

We were three days out from our battle with the *Imperious*. The captain had been out of his gourd for a moment, thinking the *Ravager* could fend off the capital ship of the region, but he had his head aright thinking our corvette could outrun their man-o'-war—'specially once he had the pilot set a course through a nearby archipelago. With our greater maneuverability and shallow draught, we could go places that big behemoth could not, and we left her behind right quick.

Once we were out of her sight, and we had the islands themselves to hide behind, Captain Torvald ordered us to double back a bit, and we skirted close to every islet and cay we passed, no matter how small, looking for any protected coves or inlets where we might put in unseen and make repairs. We'd had the *Imperious* alongside awhile during the battle, and her broadside cannons had given us a right bollocking; we'd been holed just above the waterline in two places, and *that* had been a sturdy piece of luck. The calm seas had allowed us to run, and then the glassy shallows we fled across, but any higher seas out in open water and we'd be a-heading for the bottom just as fast as you please.

We wove between those little bits of land for the better part of two days, and damned if I could tell one of 'em from another. Johnson was up in the crow, though, and 'twas he who spotted it: a tiny cove beside one of the larger jungled islands. The way the land curved about it from one side you couldn't see the damn thing from the sea, but only if you were right close to shore, which—another sturdy piece of luck—we were. We dropped anchor, tucked in there as neat as you please, and the captain chose up eleven men to go to shore with him and seek out supplies for the repairs. As ship's carpenter, I was first chosen, then Johnson, for the man had eyes that would make an eagle blink, and was a good one for spotting danger a-coming from miles off. Shartiger he took to keep the man from causing trouble in his absence—something Shartiger seemed to do as a matter of course—and the others were just beasts of burden, so far as the cap-tain was concerned: eight broad backs to carry supplies so himself wouldn't have to bend to the task.

We drove the launches up on the beach and were just preparing to strike off into the trees when the natives appeared—and appear they did, invisible even to Johnson until the jungle spat them onto the sand. Black as the tar I was to use in repairing the hull they were, and silent as shadows, just a-standing there staring as we came towards them. The captain, he told us all to be on our guard, but to wait for his signal before starting any rough stuff, and though he was a-speaking to all of us, he was staring at Shartiger when he said it. Shartiger just stared right back, fingering the hilt of his blade. We all of us had blades and guns—some more than one—but if trouble were to come, I think we were all in agreeance it would come from Shartiger, as the man seemed to carry it with him in his wallet.

Before the captain could say more, we were standing in front of the lot of 'em, and one of their number stepped forward. He was no bigger than the rest, and they were little'uns to a man, not one of 'em higher than my shoulder—they put me in mind of them pidg-i-mees I heard tell of, but if these were them, then the stories give them even shorter shrift—but from the bit of paint on his face and feathers in his hair, I took him to be their chief. Well, he shook his spear (really no more than a sharpened stick) and shouted something in his lingo. The captain looked to one of the crew he'd brought, Jean-Taunc, a black, and an island man himself, but Taunc just shrugged. "That not how they talk back home," was all he said, and the captain waved him off as useless.

Then the jungle spat out another of the little men—and this one really *was* a little man, shoulder height to the rest just as the rest were shoulder-high to us, though it may have been the little bugger's age what done that, for this one was old. His back was bent and hair grey and long, with a face so creased and weathered it looked to be made of worn and ancient rope. For all that, though, his body was lean, and arms corded with more stringy muscle than most of my hard-working shipmates. I thought I'd been mistaken when I decided the feathered one was chief, for this little man had hair a-filled with bones, as well as feathers, and though he carried no spear, there was an air of menace about him that made my guts shiver a bit, e'en though I was surrounded by my shipborne brethren.

Well, this little spider of a man scuttled up to Captain Torvald—he had an odd way of walking, a little sideways, like a crab, but he moved right quick—and started talking. Now the gibberish he was spouting didn't sound no different from the gibberish the others was spouting, but damn me if the captain didn't start nodding his head and talking back. I listened to their conversation, the two of them going back and forth, and though I couldn't understand a single word that little bastard said, I seemed to glean his bigger meaning easy enough.

The feathered one *was* their chief, and the little spider was his advisor—or something near enough as makes no never mind—and the chief wanted to know what these strange men wanted in his land. The captain let it be known that his ship had taken some damage, pointed back to the *Ravager*, and said he was a-searching for some timber with which to make repairs. The chief said, using his advisor as translator—though, still, no one but the captain was speaking a word of English—that they had lots of trees, and the strange new men could take their pick if they would but make a gift to he and his tribe.

Well, the captain tried to make payment with silver, but the chief and his advisor didn't have no idea what the coins even were; they brought out their own collection of shiny sea stones to show. He offered a flask of rum, but the chief spat his first sip out on the sand, and I didn't need no translator to tell me he wasn't for the stuff; his face squinched up even tighter than that of the wrinkled old bastard, who was watching the dickering with flat, black eyes.

Those eyes settled on the captain's cutlass, and he demanded it be brought forth. The chief was most impressed with the steel blade, and after a quick demonstration where the captain clove the head from one of the tribesman's spears with a single stroke, he proclaimed the sword to be the price for all the lumber we could carry. The captain made great ceremony of gifting his cutlass to the little king, even throwing the scabbard and belt into the bargain. I thought this an odd bit, since the captain was known to be a tight one with the purse strings, but when the chief, grinning and swiping his new blade through the air to hear the sound, invited us all to his village for a meal in our honor, Captain Torvald's grin mirrored his own.

With loud voice he told us all we were to follow the chief and his men to their village, where we would feast and be on our best behaviour, but through surreptitious hand motions, he signaled us to be close to our weapons and on our guard and to await his signal—and again he paid special attention to Shartiger on this bit—before any hard action.

We followed the little men through the jungle to the clearing where they'd made their village; not more than a collection of rude huts and lean-tos, really, but it was what they were gathered around that grabbed my attention and held it hard. 'Twas a tree, the like of which I'd never seen.

We'd been walking amongst trees I'd seen before, though knew not much of, having never used them for aught but to patch hulls shattered by cannon and reef, and usually pressed for time at that. But this… God's blood, this was different. The great trunk was wider than a half dozen men abreast and taller by half than the jungle trees about it. The limbs spread so wide I saw they had caused the clearing to be, its leaves—the littlest wider than both my hands together—blotting out the sun for its much shorter brethren and causing them to die off. "What is *that*," I whispered, not even really knowing I was speaking, but suddenly the spider was standing at my elbow, staring at me with those damned eyes of his. I realized then they were the most spiderish thing about him; sure, he might have had a bent back and knotted, spindly limbs and a scuttly way of moving, but those black eyes were shiny and flat, and even this close, I couldn't see any whites. Well, it almost unmanned me to have them a-staring at me from less than an arm's length away.

He pinned me with those hateful eyes as he reached out and took the captain by the elbow. He pulled Torvald closer—no mean feat, for the captain was twice his size and not an easy man to move in the best of times—and pointed to the great tree with his free hand. Again, nothing but gibberish poured out of his mouth, but we had no doubt as to what his message was: we could take our timber from any tree but *that* tree. *That* one we were not to touch.

The little bugger spun away from us, leaving the captain and me to look at the tree, and then each other. My face probably showed the relief I felt at having a little distance between me and the evil little sod, but the captain just looked curious. "I think there's more of a story there," he said to me. "What do you think?" But then he, too, spun away before I could make an answer, off to take part in the planning of the festivities, or so it seemed at the time.

It wasn't 'til the feast was about to begin that I realized there were but nine of us there what came on the *Ravager*. I looked about, afeared, for alongside stories of the pidge-i-mees I'd heard tell of savages who eat men, and if that was the kind of feast we'd be sitting down to, then I was for fleeing. But the captain saw my concern and reassured me in a voice meant to carry that he'd sent the three back to look after the ship. Well, this was a bit of tomfoolery, as the *Ravager* was a-crewed by seventy-six souls—seventy-eight, if Eckhart and Monroe pulled through, wounded against the *Imperious*—and in my mind that left sixty-four to look after the ship while we was a-land. But the captain's hands told a different story, signing again to keep my weapons ready while adding an admonishment to keep my gob shut.

We sat down to the meal—I didn't recognize the meat, so I stuck to the fruits, just in case—and it was an odd time. It was a friendly thing, but none of us could speak to a one of them save the spider, and he was kept hopping translating between the chief and the captain. I noticed Jean-Taunc skulking about the outskirts of the gathering and not eating—an odd thing for him. I made my way over and asked what was the matter. He rolled his big eyes at me, showing me their whites, and indicated the spider. "That one," he said, "he's not just an advisor. My people have ones like that. He is their priest, their medicine man, and he uses magic. Oh, I have a bad feeling 'bout this." He rolled his eyes again, as if looking for a way to flee.

I started to ask him about the magic he spoke of, but just then the captain asked a question that caught my attention, and from the way my seven shipmates quieted down—even that big bastard Shartiger—it caught their attention as well.

"We're all impressed by this great tree you have, and from your prohibition, we know of its importance to you. Can you tell us a bit about it, if you don't mind? I know we're all curious."

Well, the chief and his advisor spoke a moment, and then the spider strode up before all the seated folk and stood straight—well, as straight as he could—and looked each and every one of us in the eye. It made me shiver, having him glare at me like that, especially after Taunc's talk of magic. Then he started in with his tale of the tree, and though it was long, and accompanied by much gesticulation, again I got the gist of it without understanding a word—and now Taunc's talk of magic was a-picking at my mind the whole time.

What I understood was that long ago, when the tribe was but a single family, they had been in trouble. Demons of the jungle, animals, maybe another tribe, I'm not certain, but something was killing them off and they couldn't defend themselves, so they were running. They ran until they found a clearing—*the* clearing—and the great tree. With the bulk of its trunk to set their backs against, they managed to fight off what was a-following. More than that, they defeated it. Knowing a good thing when it was staring them in the face, they built a home there and then, and beneath the tree they thrived. The width of the clearing allowed them to see things a-coming, and the tree itself protected them to one side. The fruit of the tree fed them when game was scarce, and they made weapons from its fallen limbs, spears that were harder and sharper than anything they'd had before.

Then the tree came to one of their number in his dreams, talking to him and suchlike, telling him it was the god of their island and that it would care for and protect them for as long as they worshipped it. Well, they struck a bargain that very night. From that time on the family grew, eventually becoming the tribe of dozens we now saw, and the descendants of that tree-talker were tree-talkers themselves, advisors to the chiefs to a man. And that was why the current tree-talker—the spider—had told us not to touch the tree. They might collect the fallen branch now and again, but they would never take from the living tree, as that would be harming their god.

The spider stared straight at the captain as he made this point, much the way the captain sometimes stared at Shartiger. For his part, Captain Torvald spread his hands in a gesture of innocence—but dropped them suddenly in a sign I recognized.

The jungle about us erupted with men, what looked to be the entire crew of the *Ravager* flooding into the clearing at a dead run, guns a-blasting. All about me tribesmen were falling, and those who weren't falling were screaming in panic. None of them had ever seen a gun before, hadn't even recognized them though we'd carried them openly, and the sound and smoke amidst the fury of the charge had them terrified almost to madness. I saw the chief, frightened but determined, brandish his new sword against the captain. Torvald, though, merely drew and shot, sending a ball into the chief's chest that sent the man tumbling and had him dead before he hit the ground.

I'd been slow to tip to it, so caught up in the old man's story had I been, but the captain had sent those three men back to the *Ravager* not to help look after her, but to fetch his crew. 'Twas a thing he'd done before, for morale: following a defeat the likes of which we'd faced against the *Imperious*, Captain Torvald always chose us an easy target, and that day he'd chosen the little village under the great spreading tree.

Though the villagers outnumbered us, surprise and firepower were on our side, and it was a slaughter. More than half their number were women and children, and those fled into the jungle even faster than the menfolk, though I saw Shartiger catch hold of a young lady even as the attack was going on, dragging her off to the nearest of the huts to begin his raping to the music of powder and shot and blood.

Some of the crew gave chase as the savages fled, but I was of a better mind than to try to follow them through the jungle. Instead, I walked about the village looking at the dead. Not searching 'em, mind, but looking. I wasn't even sure what I was a-searching *for*, not until Jean-Taunc walked past, eyes still showing white with fear, and said, "You won't find him here." I knew who he was talking about straight off, and he was right: I'd been looking for the spider without even realizing it.

He was also right that I didn't find him; the evil-eyed advisor had legged it, scuttling away through the trees.

Shortly after this realization, I heard a hard crash, and me and some of the other crew all went a-running. We found Captain Torvald with three other men, all standing at the foot of the great tree, gathered around a felled limb. The branch was huge, thicker at the base than I am wide, the white knob of the cut end oozing dark, reddish stuff that I first took to be blood, though it turned out to be merely dark sap. The spider's so recently told story in mind, I just stared for a minute, more than a little stunned. The captain saw me gawping and called out to me.

"What do you think, there, Tim," said he. "Wouldn't having an island god for a figurehead be a spot of luck?" One of the balls from the *Imperious* had taken our old figurehead clean away, and there had been much grumbling about it from the crew, those superstitious bastards saying the man-o'-war had shot off our luck. Torvald was asking me loudly, and in front of the crew, and I understood what he was about, even without his eyes boring into mine to tell me I better answer rightly if I knew what was good for me.

"Oh, aye, sir," I said, "a great spot of luck, I should imagine," though I left off that I wasn't sure it was *good* luck 'twould be bringing.

Three days we spent in that clearing beneath the tree. On the first, I supervised the rip-cutting of some trees for planking, and then the setting, pegging, and tarring the lot to patch the breaches in the ship's hull. Leaving the tar to set and dry for two days, I took to fashioning the god-tree limb into a figure to mount to the prow. Two days wasn't enough time to do more than get the thing started—once the bark was off, the wood proved to be whiter than the lightest pine, though harder than teak, and not easy to work—but that was all the captain would give me. Though he never mentioned it, I was of the opinion he was as afeared of the spider as I was, and was eager to escape the little witch doctor's reach. I did notice that, though most of the men spent some time in the village, dallying with an island woman or two—except for Shartiger, who enjoyed practices too vile for most quayside doxies and seemed bent on working his way through *all* of them—the captain retired immediately to the ship and ne'er set foot on the island again.

After two days of working on her, the captain ordered me to peg what I had up in place of the old girl we had lost. The crew's grumbling grew worse when they saw what we'd be setting sail behind: a crude figure, pale and unfinished, with only the roughest of features. The captain shouted over the lot of them, wearing as deliberate a grin as ever I've seen and saying as how I'd now get to finish the figure on the sea. "Shaping our luck as we go," was how he put it, though from his glassy stare as he took the thing in, I'd wager he was regretting his decision to leave so soon. No help for it, though; he needed to get the crew away from those island ladies before the bunch refused to go.

The sun was bright and the breezes warm as we weighed anchor and set the *Ravager* a-dancing across the waves once more. My patch in the prow was holding up just fine, and the longer the tar had to set the tighter she'd be. The crew's spirits rose considerably as they took this all in, and many a shout and a *yo-ho* could be heard as we made our way once around the bay and tacked out towards the open sea. They rose—but only 'til we reached the mouth of the cove, a narrow channel with rocks to one side and a cliff to the other. As we approached, the crow—Johnson again—cried out and pointed, and we saw the spider waiting for us atop the cliff.

The spindly little bugger was dancing and leaping about, and the wind carried his singing voice to us. I got no meaning from his words this time, but his tone was filled with menace. Several of the crew, led by Shartiger, started shooting at him, but he paid them no mind as lead balls whizzed through the air about him and crashed into the cliff beneath his naked feet. Just as the ship passed through the gap and we were as close to the little man as we were to get, he stooped suddenly to scoop up a spear and let fly at the *Ravager*. Shartiger, who had crowded right into the prow to get a better shot at the savage, saw the spear coming and threw up a hand to ward it off. The sharpened stick went straight through his palm, nailing him to my rough figurehead with a sound like thunder.

All eyes had followed the throw, and by the time we'd all seen Shartiger's fate and looked back, the cliff head was empty. The captain barked orders to the pilot to steer clear of the cliff, wary of more spears to follow, but there were none. The *Ravager* made it out to sea without further molestation, accompanied by Shartiger's screams as we wiggled loose the spear, sunk uncommon deep into that figurehead, having no choice but to widen his wound as we worked. He'd passed out by the time we were done, and I left a mate belowdecks trying to bandage his hand before he woke.

When I got back up in the sun, Captain Torvald was addressing the crew from the quarterdeck, waxing poetical about our escapades on the island and referring to Shartiger as "our single casualty of war." Well, I could see he was worried about morale again, and I took it upon myself to go clean our man's blood from what was supposed to be our lucky figurehead before talk of blood and bad luck could start up. When I got there, though, I thought at first that someone'd been there before me, for there was no blood on my carving. There was still blood on the deck, though, and the rail at the figure's feet, and any man of our crew knew that to do a job as half-arsed as that would fetch him a right flogging.

When I set my eye closer to my work, I noted a darkening of the white wood in all the places blood would've flowed, almost as if the figurehead had soaked it in like a sponge. I noticed, too, and this with a shock, that the deep gouge made by the spearhead was gone as well, the figure's side unmarred, though still rough-hewn.

Not wanting to volunteer for a flogging myself, I set about cleaning all trace of the blood from the deck and rail even as behind me the captain was doing his best to beguile the crew into forgetting all about it. Just as I finished, Johnson shouted down from the crow's nest again. I looked where he was pointing as the captain's voice died. Dead ahead, in the middle of a bright, sunny day, was a fog bank so thick it looked like a wall rising out of the sea.

The captain called up to Johnson to ask if there was a way around the bank, but Johnson shouted that it stretched as far as he could see in either direction and seemed to be moving towards us to boot. Of choices we now had three: we could continue on into the fog, hoping it was a narrow bank, drop anchor and wait for it to pass, or turn back towards the island the captain had just been bragging about leaving behind. I was thinking we'd drop anchor, but the captain wanted to be a man of action, so we trimmed the sails, reduced speed, and into the fog we went.

The *Ravager* had been sailing due west and straight out towards open ocean, but the waters were unknown to us. The captain ordered Johnson out of the crow and into the prow, setting old sharp-eyes to watch for rock and reef, and men were stationed both port and starboard to keep watch for rocks and work the sounders. The crew went about their business in silence, the better to hear any warnings from

Johnson and the sounders, and it went on that way for what felt like the better part of a day, though in all that gray and with no sun to set against the yardarm, time became a funny thing. The mist was thick and clinging and smelled like vegetables that had been left too long and begun to rot, and the ship's morale, what had been on the climb until Shartiger was struck down, and then again until the fog came, had taken a serious downward turn. It was into all this timeless silence that the screams came.

Men were crowded into the sleeping quarters by the time I made my way below, but I rode the captain's wake as he elbowed his way through. Shartiger had been bound into his hammock, the whole thing wrapped closed with rope, leaving naught but his head and wounded arm protruding from one end like the foot of a clam. His hand was swollen like a bladder, and he was alternately flailing about with it as he struggled in his confinement and holding it as far from him as he could, screaming and staring at it in what looked to be absolute terror. The crewman I'd left trying to bandage that hand was standing by, gripping another length of rope and breathing hard, a blackened eye and swollen cheek testament to his unsuccessful attempts to bind that free arm to Shartiger's side.

The captain ordered men to help tie that arm, then bellowed for us to get back to our posts. We all filed out, but not before Shartiger had another bout of screaming at his hand—and this time there were words mixed in with all the screaming. It was words, for sure, but I couldn't make out a one of 'em; I'd listened to the spider telling his whole story of the tree, not understanding a word of it, and if I'da been pressed, I'd have said Shartiger was screaming at his hand in that same savage lingo, though the man had never spoken a word of anything but English.

I'd just regained the fog-filled deck when there came another scream, this one long and bloodcurdling and from somewhere towards the front of the ship. The foul mist was so thick I couldn't *see* but half the ship in a single go anymore, and I started forward, wondering aloud what had gone wrong now and muttering that things really couldn't get much worse. I should have kept my gob shut, as just then the *Ravager* ground to a sudden halt, sending myself and the rest of the crew tumbling across the main deck. I fetched up hard against the rise for the forecastle with the wind beaten out of me and feeling the luckier for it: three men I saw meet with the mainmast mid-tumble, each of them breaking at least one bone, and for one of them—the mate, a small man with a big voice—it was his neck.

The captain came roaring up from below—he'd been caught within the narrow confines of the belowdecks stairs, and had managed to come through without a lengthy tumble—and practically flew past me and up to the forecastle, a-frothing at the mouth and screaming Johnson's name. I scrambled to my feet to follow and caught up with Torvald in the prow, leaning over the low rail and shouting into the fog. I drew up alongside him and looked down over the rail.

"Sandbar," I said, for that it was, the *Ravager's* bow sunk into it like a sailor's nose nestled between a doxie's dugs. We'd run hard aground, and it was a lucky thing we'd not been under full sail. As it was, I'd have to run below and check my patching to see if any of the new tar had sprung.

"Yes, a sandbar, that's right," shouted Captain Torvald, rounding on me. "The very thing Johnson was a-setting here to spot! Eagle-eye my arse—closed-eye, more like! If he fell asleep at his post then like as not he fell over onto the bar." Here he faced out to the fog again, voice rising to earsplitting, leaning on the rail to cast his words with everything he had. "And if he *is* out on that bar, he best just start swimming now because he's not getting back on *my* ship!" He turned and pointed a finger at me. "And if he's still on this ship, I want him found and brought to me. You hear me? Brought to me!"

I heard the words, but all I could do was stare at the captain's hand. "Captain," I said, pointing. "Look." As the captain spread his fingers and gawped at them, I looked at the rail, then the deck, bending close to better see through the ever-thickening fog.

Blood. The rail was spattered with it, the deck awash in it. The capstan looked to be half-painted red. We hadn't noticed, the deck already fog-slick and the rotting stink of the mucky mist covering the hot-metal smell of it, but we were standing in the midst of a huge red stain. "Sir," I said, "that scream right before we hit. Do you think that might've been…"

The captain yanked a kerchief from his sleeve and began wiping the blood from his hands, saying "Must have been, must have been. But what the devil happened to him?"

"Don't know, sir," says I, looking about for some hint of Johnson other than his blood…and that was when I saw the figurehead. We were standing right aside it, just as Johnson would have to watch the water, and the rail all about it had been splashed...but the feet of my figure were as white and unsullied as when I'd carved 'em. They were just atop the rail and should've been at least dotted, but I didn't see a drop—not until I looked up at the hands, and then the prickles set into me and the hairs on the back of my neck stood tall. Pressed back to its sides like a soldier at attention, those hands were as red as the mark of Shartiger's blood from the spider's spear, the stain sunk into the wood itself again, no actual blood still marring the surface.

Jean-Taunc's words leaped to my mind, and I remembered his frightened, rolling eyes as he told me the advisor was a man of magic. With shaking hand I pointed the reddened fingers out to the captain, asking what he thought it was about. He stared awhile, and I watched his face go as wooden as that of the figurehead itself. "Nothing," he finally said. "It means nothing."

"But Captain, Taunc said—" I started, but he stepped up close to hiss right in my face.

"It means nothing I tell you—and if I hear of you showing this *nothing* to another of the crew, then I'll send you down to keep Johnson company in hell, and I promise you that." He took a little step back and looked about. "Now, you get a couple of the crew and swab this deck, and choose a pair that know how to shut their gobs. I want it all gone, and I don't want a lot of loose talk about it. I'll be trying to get my ship off this damnable bar."

He strode off, already shouting orders, and I started to move down the other side of the ship—and almost ran straight into Jean-Taunc, who loomed out of the fog right in front of me. "Damn me, but you gave me a turn," I said. "Be a good man and grab yourself a mop and—" But he wasn't even looking at me, just staring over my shoulder towards the figurehead, the white wood of it invisible in the fog.

"I told you," he whispered. "Black magic." Then he walked away, leaving me alone in the prow and not pleased about it. I hunted through the fog for a couple of likely swabbies and set them to work on the deck while I went into the hold to check on my repairs, taking my time examining the strained tar for signs of likely leakage; I didn't know what was going on, but the longer I was down there, the longer I'd be away from that red-handed thing carved from sacred wood.

The sun was going down by the time I got back up on deck—or the fog had started getting darker as well as thicker. The captain had spent his time having the crew shift any cargo as rearward as possible, then having the crew itself gather in the stern, hoping to raise the bow and loosen the *Ravager* from the bar's grip. When that didn't work, he had them shuffling port and starboard, trying to rock the ship free. When he had no luck there—and after the forecastle deck had been cleaned, I was sure—he sent the stouter of the men out onto the bar itself to try to push us free while the others gathered again in the stern, but as the day grew dim and night approached, the *Ravager* still sat aground in the middle of the water. Without a stronger tide than we'd seen that day, or mayhap a storm to stir up waves enough to lift the ship free, we were staying put, and though the captain was all confident smiles and back slaps to the crew, when I asked about I found he'd stayed in the rear of the ship the whole day and not approached the prow after leaving me there to swab the deck. Johnson, he'd explained just as he had to me, had fallen asleep at his post and been cast overboard when we met the bar, and of bloodstains and figure-heads he made no mention.

The captain retired to his cabin at sundown, proclaiming to any who might listen that he wanted privacy in which to contemplate our predicament and think of a solution. He ordered a night watch, including someone in the crow's nest, for, as he said, we were in the open in unknown waters and, should the fog away, we could be at the mercy of any ship to come along, and the captain of the *Imperious* might be holding a grudge.

Well, the men chosen for watch all grumbled heartily about not being able to see two yards together through the fog, and that was passing true. This was the thickest sea fog I'd ever been in, and the dark worsened things; it was impossible to make out anything more than shapes farther than a man-length away. Figgis, the second mate—now the first mate, promotion having occurred with the breaking of the old mate's neck as we'd run aground—listened to their complaints, as did we all, and then set them about their task, saying as how they'd signed the articles, so would do their jobs. There was no carousing that night belowdecks, all of us aware sound more'n sight was what was important now, and we all turned in, determined to get ourselves free of the sand and out of the fog the next morning.

The thud woke me more'n the scream, though there were those what heard both. All had heard it, and all were awake, but 'twas naught but me and Tomlin, the bosun, who ran for the deck. I looked back, but all my mates, men I'd felt protected by when we met the savages and their tree-talker, they all looked away but Jean-Taunc. The islander just rolled his eyes at me again, shook his head, and jerked his chin towards Schartiger. The big man was still wrapped securely in his hammock, but he wasn't asleep; his eyes were wide, head jerking from side to side as he muttered constantly. He wasn't screaming anymore, but the crew had gone so quiet I could hear him all the way across the cabin, and the words spilling non-stop from his lips were more of that what sounded like the spider's lingo. I looked to Jean-Taunc, but the bastard just shook his head again.

"Magic," he said, and I turned to follow the bosun. The rest of the crew might've heard Taunc speaking of magic, but they hadn't seen Johnson's blood on the deck, nor the stains in the wood of the figurehead. They might've felt safer down there, away from the fog, but I'd started to think being able to run away might be a good thing right about then, and there was only so much room belowdecks to run in.

There was a commotion as I came out onto the deck; it was harder than ever to see through the damned fog, and I nearly ran into Tomlin's back. Someone was holding him at swordpoint, the two of them shouting. The swordsman bore a lantern, but all it did was turn the fog whiter, and it was only by his voice that I recognized him as Figgis, the new first mate.

"What goes here," I cried, and the bosun quieted.

The mate, though, kept brandishing his blade. "There was a yell whilst I was on guard," says he, "and I caught this bastard a-sneaking through the soup!"

"We all heard the yell," I replied, "and the bang. It shook us awake below to a man. He"—here I clapped a hand to Tomlin's back—"was below, with us, and come a-running at the noise, like me."

"Where are the rest?" said Figgis, looking over my shoulder.

"They've jelly for guts," says I. "We're better off not having them underfoot. Now, who was it a-screaming in the night? Do you know?"

His shape in the mist shrugged its shoulders. "Not sure," he said, motioning for us to follow. "Who did you set in the nest?"

"Greenley," answered the bosun. "He mayn't have eyes like Johnson, but he's a good man in a pinch."

"Remember you said that," said the Figgis, a-hunkering down by a low pile of something on the deck, holding the lantern close. "I didn't recognize him without them, but as you can see, Greenley don't have eyes like anyone anymore."

There was an eddy in the murk, and for just a moment I saw the shape clearly, and if it *was* Greenley I saw the mate's difficulty immediately. Greenley's eyes were gone, the scooping of them having torn great strips down his face, his cheeks all turned inside out and hanging like tongues from the sides of his jaw.

Well, I hadn't supped on much that night, but I hurried to the rail to set what I'd 'et free again as Tomlin managed to gag down his rising gorge.

"Now that don't look like it happened in the fall," said Figgis. "That looks like someone done that. I have to fetch the captain." His voice was steady, but in the lamplight, I saw his hand a-shaking as he pointed to the bosun. "You come with me. You"—and here the trembling finger pointed at me—"go tell the men to stay below."

I'd have told him there was nary a chance of any of that lot stepping foot on the deck until the sun had burned off the cursed fog, but my stomach heaved again, and all I could do was motion them on as I retched. The pair hurried off, the brume and dark swallowing all sign of the lamp right quick.

I was just catching my breath when yet another scream cut the night. I wheeled towards the sound and the fog grew suddenly lighter, as if the sun were rising, but from the wrong direction. I had started towards the light when Tomlin staggered out of the gloom and right into me, sending us both crashing to the deck.

"It took him! It took him!" the man screamed, and in the growing light I could make out the width of his eyes, and if they opened any further he'd have wound up a match for Greenley.

"What took him?" I cried, scrambling to my feet and hoisting the man up. "What do you mean? What took him?"

"I don't *know*," he wailed. "I didn't *see*! We were heading aft to fetch the captain when something loomed out of the fog and…and just *took* him!"

I was watching the fog grow brighter by the moment. "What's that light, then?" I asked.

"The lantern fell when it took him—it was so *fast*—and there was a splash of oil and the flash of flame and—"

I gripped him hard by the vest and roared into his face. "Do you mean to tell me the ship's afire?" All the simpleton could do was nod before I cast him aside and raced for the quarters. The light in the fog had begun to go all flickery, and the scent of burning creosote was shouldering its way through the damp stink. I roused the men—no one ignores the cry aboard ship when that cry is fire—and set them to work bucketing up seawater to douse the flames. The lamp had set the edge of the quarter deck ablaze, then the listing ship had let the oil flow over the side and down the hull, spreading the flames as it went. The aftward of my two patches was alight, and that'd play havoc on the new tar, but none of that would matter if the *Ravager* burned to the waterline.

"The captain!" I cried. "Where's the captain?" The whole crew was at work, half hoisting up water with rope and bucket, the other half running to throw it on the flames. The men were terrified, for we'd not done a thing with Greenley, and the bosun was telling anyone who'd listen about the taking of the mate, but they worked like dogs in their fear. Within minutes there was no sign of the near conflagration other than a blackening of the deck and the stink of the thing. I looked about for Tomlin, but he was amidst a growing crowd of our shipmates, all gathering close in the brume and plenty near to hear as he kept repeating "It took him! I don't know, it just took him!" Well, he didn't sound right in the head to me, and the first mate was gone, and what with the second mate becoming first mate right afore his disappearance, I wasn't even sure we had another second mate yet. I asked every man I found about the captain: not a one had seen or heard him, though everyone else but Shartiger seemed to be on deck.

Choosing a couple of men at random—I didn't much care who they were, just so long as I didn't have to move through that damn fog alone—I took a lantern and we went to Captain Torvald's quarters, all of us by then aware that this was the errand that had lost us the mate. I was a-thinking of how the captain had avoided the scene of Johnson's apparent demise and then retired early from the fog, and wondering if we'd find the man huddled in his cabin and not wanting to come out. It was a thing that could bleed the courage right out of a crew, a captain losing his nerve, and I was wishing I'd been a little more discriminating at my choice in companions for this venture, neither man accompanying me being known for their discretion. Then we reached the captain's door, and I saw I needn't have worried. Not about that, anyway.

The door hung loose on a single hinge, the top one torn right from the hull, as was the plate of the still-thrown bolt. Inside we found no sign of the captain, only signs of struggle: broken bottles, a chair smashed to kindling, and—worst of all—the ship's sextant bent into uselessness. And the blood, o' course.

'Twas Babbage first saw the blood—slipped in it, really—and with a cry he took off into the fog, either to alert the men or a-running for his own berth. I ordered the other swab, Thompson by name, to stand fast as I looked at the blood, trying to read the signs. I could see it here and there amidst the carnage, but in the last, it appeared to lead through the broken door and out onto the deck, the very swath Babbage had slipped in.

"It's got him, ain't it, Carpenter?" said Thompson.

"What's got who?" I replied, my head still awhirl with what we'd found—and *not* found. "The captain, you mean? What are you on about?"

"You know," he said, rolling his eyes like Jean-Taunc. "The thing what took Figgis. I heard what Tomlin was saying about it—we all heard—the thing in the fog."

I told him he needed to shut his mouth—ordered him, really, though I had no authority, I was just ship's carpenter—and we went back to tell the crew the captain was gone, though I figured Babbage was already hard at work on that. Most of the crew was still milling about by the scorched deck, all the usual work of running a ship at sea taken care of by the sand what still held us tight as a miser's fist.

"Where's Babbage?" I said to the first bloke I saw.

"Babbage?" says he. "I thought he was with you."

"We parted by the captain's quarters," I said, relieved I might be able to tell of the captain without Babbage talking about buckets of blood. "He must've gone down to his berth."

"I just come from there," said one of the shapes in the fog, though I couldn't make out who. "I went to check on Shartiger. He's still down there a-talking nonsense and being louder about it now, but I didn't see sign of Babbage."

"Huh," I said, not asking the man but more thinking out loud. "I wonder where he's got to, then?"

E'en as I said it, I knew 'twas a mistake, but it was too late. "It took him!" the bosun cried. Those about him with lanterns raised them high, but he backed away from the light. "The thing in the fog, it took Babbage!"

"Stop your noise," I shouted. The men what I could see had drawn closer together, had started to have a huddled look about them, and I knew I had to get the man to stop his fear-mongering before he set a panic into the superstitious crew. "There ain't nothing in the fog that ain't supposed to be there."

"Where's the captain?" piped up a voice in the crowd. "He'll know what to do, right? You went to get him, Carpenter! Where is he?"

I tried to grip Thompson's arm in warning, but I'd not been paying attention and let the man get out of reach. "Cap'n's gone," he shouted.

"Shut your gob!" I hissed, but he never even heard me.

"His cabin door's burst," Thompson shouted. "Furniture all smashed to bits and blood on the walls! On the *walls*!" he said again, as if they wouldn't have heard him the first time.

All about me rose up frightened mutterings, but one voice rose above the rest. "It took him!" screamed the bosun, backing farther from the lights, just an arm-waving shape in the mist. "It took the captain! Took him away into the fog!"

"Now just hold on, damn you," I bellowed, and Tomlin went silent. I snatched one of the lanterns and strode forwards, wanting to confront the man in front of the crew and quash the terror I could feel spreading through the ranks. "We don't know what happened to the captain," I said, raising my lantern as I closed in on him. "But there's nothing in this fog that shouldn't be—"

I drew up short. I'd reached the rail—nearly gutted myself on it in the mist—but there was no sign of the bosun. I looked left and right along the ship, but though men loomed out of the fog in either direction, none of them was the man I sought. "Where did he go?" I said, but even as the words left my lips I knew, and the hairs rose up once more on the back of my neck.

"It took him!" someone shouted, and the words spread through the crew faster than plague through a slum. "It took him," they cried. "The thing in the fog!"

There was a sudden scream, and the men around me, already round-eyed with superstitious fear, seemed to go mad. They ran about, fighting each other, every man intent on getting to another part of the ship and determined not to be the one left behind in the fog. Them that bore blades slashed at any shape that came towards them through the mist, uncaring whether they struck friend or foe, just so long as they struck first. Men fell all about, kicking across the deck with their guts hanging out as other men ran past, wildly swinging at eddies in the mist and shipmates alike.

The screaming, the blood, the confusion, it all put me in mind of the attack on the village, though even the confusion on the island had had a bit of an "us-and-them" feel to it; here, it was every man for himself. That thought of the island put another image in my head: the spider, telling his story of the tribe and their tree, and that lingo of his a-floating across the clearing, making sense without words, while Jean-Taunc's eyes rolled and he spoke of magic.

That lingo of his…

Shartiger! I thought. *The spider marked him with that spear, and the man's been down there muttering in that native gibberish since all this began!*

I don't know bollocks about magic, but a connection's a connection is the way I see it. I drew my knife, just in case, and stayed by the rail as I made my way through the mad battle so no one could come upon me from behind as I headed for the crew's quarters. Shartiger was alone down there when I arrived, everyone else being up on deck and swinging at shadows. That swab from the crew had spoken aright: the big man was still bound into his hammock like a fish in a tight net, but what I'd last heard as muttering had grown to almost a shout. It was the spider's words in Shartiger's voice, and just hearing it turned my spine to ice.

"Shartiger," I shouted, but he just kept talking. I moved closer, raising my voice, trying to drown him out. "Shartiger, you shut your trap! Shut it now, I'm warning you!" Only a single lamp was lit, and as I drew nearer, I saw through the shadows that Shartiger's eyes were closed like a man asleep, though the cords stood out in his bull neck from the effort of the constant chant. My knife was still in hand from my trip through the fighting, and now I raised it. "Last chance, man! I'm warning you!"

Shartiger had but to open his eyes to see the threat, but his lids never flickered. Instead his voice rose, flinging those words at me even louder until I reached down and, with a stroke like I was opening a bluefish's belly, slit his throat almost back to the neck bone. Now I may've been a pirate, but I'd never slit a man's gullet before, and I wasn't prepared for the gout of blood what came out, spraying across my face and neck. The stuff hit me like a hot slap, but even as the big man struggled against his ropes and fell still, I reveled in the silence that filled the cabin when that gabbling mouth of his stopped its working. I believe I even smiled a bit.

Then his eyes opened.

It weren't his lids fluttering, or relaxing, or even anything like that death-spasm you hear tell about. They snapped open, wide open, and Shartiger wasn't looking up at me with his own piggy little eyes; these were flat and black, and even in the dim of the single lamp I could see that, wide as they were open, there weren't a hint of a white to be seen. They were the spider's eyes, and they fixed upon me with a hatred that brought back my spine of ice and nearly had the piss trickling down my leg. I froze in the act of sleeving some of his blood from my cheeks, but I staggered back when his lips twisted into a grin, wide and savage, and the chant started anew—but not from his mouth. The smile still stretched his face, but the wound, the wound in his throat where I had cut his head half off…it *moved.* It *writhed*, the gaping edges forming the words as ragged bits of flesh and gristle fluttered in his breath, and the spider's own voice came out of the dead man's throat!

I fled, the spider's chant swelling to fill the room behind me, nearly pushing me up the stairs. I burst out onto the deck, remembering at the last that there was a pitched battle raging across the planks…but all I saw about me was fog, with not a sound but the chant rising up from the quarters. A hollow thud came from my right, and I ran that way, stumbling over bodies as I went—men I knew, but I didn't give them more than a glance as I tried not to catch my toes.

A sudden shape came at me and I leaped back, barely avoiding a swinging belaying pin. "What are you about?" I cried, and Knobby Buckman drew up short.

"Oh, it's you, Carp," said the little man, looking positively weepy with relief. "I thought you was the thing! Come, help me with this."

I might have made an answer, but my mind was still reeling with memories of the dead man talking in the spider's voice. He took my arm and pulled me to the rail, where I saw he'd been trying to lower one of the launch boats, running back and forth between the winches. Before I could ask him where the hell he thought he was going, he started babbling at me in a voice filled with terror.

"I seen it! I seen the thing in the fog! All that fighting, the men killing each other—that weren't for me, Carp, and 'tweren't for Tucker neither. We stayed at the rail and moved away from the fighting, just hoping to stay alive. Tuck wanted to run, but he couldn't swim, so we started for the boats—and that's when it got him! He weren't but an arm's length away, and I seen it come out of the fog, a big man shape, but not a man! I seen its face. Like something from hell! It grabbed him, and they disappeared into the fog, and I heard him screaming. Carp, I heard Tuck scream—"

Arms shot about him from behind the man, closing about him in a great wrestler's hug. Buckman's eyes went wide, mouth opening in a scream, and he reached for me, but it was too late. With a backward jerk, he disappeared into the fog, and nothing touched me but his screams, which grew loud and shrill and—stopped.

I hadn't had a chance to help, the attack had been so quick, but I couldn't have anyway, rooted to the spot by what I'd seen. Just as Buckman was yanked out of sight, a face had appeared, winking through the mist above his head for an instant, but an instant was all I'd needed to recognize it: those blank eyes, mere lump of a nose, and rough, unfinished mouth. O'course I recognized it! It was the face I'd carved in-to the figure made from the savages' sacred wood, then pegged to the prow of the *Ravager*!

Jean-Taunc's voice flitted through my head, speaking the word *magic*, and in an instant I remembered that Shartiger wasn't the only one marked by the spider's spear: the big man had been nailed to the new figurehead in a connection borne of blood and pain forged by a weapon made from the same sacred tree. The spider's voice came to me then, rising up through the stairway from a dead man's throat, and I was stabbing and sawing at the hawser securing the front of the launch before I even knew what I was about.

The rope was thick and felt like iron beneath my fingers, but my knife was sharp, and the strands were already parting when I heard the heavy thud. And then another.

And another.

I knew what it was, and the thought spurred me on, working my blade against the twisted hemp like a man gone mad—which I may have been. Johnson, Greenley, the mate, the captain—no man had killed these men, though dead they were. Like Buckman, they'd been slain by a thing of black magic and revenge, brought to life somehow through Shartiger's blood and the spider's hate, hate I'd seen in a dead man's eyes, and just as it had come for them, those footsteps in the fog said it was coming for me.

Another heavy, wood-on-wood thunk sounded right behind me as the damn hawser finally snapped and the nose of the launch boat fell free and swung down against the *Ravager*'s hull with a bang I felt in my feet, dangling only by its stern rope. I dashed away from the thing I felt so close behind, sprinting forward to the rail pulley holding that second rope as yet another hollow thud came through the fog, and still another, the thing stalking me picking up speed as it came. I reached up and attacked the rope, sawing at it two-handed, the fear sounds from my own throat nearly drowning out the evil chant coming from below.

I felt another thud in my feet and couldn't be sure whether it was the launch swinging 'gainst the hull again or the tread of the spider's wooden devil closing in. I felt it again, too rhythmical, too close to be anything but the footfall of my doom drawing near, when the full weight of the launch against the single rope caused the half-cut hawser to part with a twang. The launch crashed to the sea just as the rope, stretched to its utmost by the weight of the boat, snapped back towards the winch like a heavy hemp bullwhip. Had I been a taller man, like Shartiger or Captain Torvald, it might've taken my head clean off. As it was, I lost some hair and blood at its passage, though I didn't know it at the time. All I knew was that just behind me the heavy whip struck something with a hearty whack, and I heard the thud-thud of heavy, stumbling wooden feet, and I was a-diving over the side, just praying to anyone who'd listen that I didn't land headfirst on the launch or dive straight onto the sandbar and break my neck.

I went deep enough to touch the sand, but there was water enough to break my fall, and for another piece of luck the launch hadn't landed downside up nor smashed itself on the bar. I scrambled aboard, shipped the oars, and started rowing for all I was worth. I didn't care whether I was heading out to open sea or back towards the spider's island, not so long as I was heading away from that ship where a demon walked and the dead spoke and neither could be stopped.

In minutes I was out of the fog, and I can't tell you how my spirits lifted to see the stars and breathe clean sea air once more. I took a bearing from the pole star as best I could, put that cursed grey wall behind me, and set to pulling that launch away from the *Ravager* and the island both, determined at that moment to row all the way back to England if I could but find my way.

O'course, by morning I realized I'd set out with no provisions or—even worse—water, and that England was an impossibility, but I thought to find another island, one without a spider of its own. Four days later—at least, I believe it was four days—I was picked up by your lordship and the crew of the *Imperious*. You arrested me for piracy and demanded my confession, and now you have it. Now, milord, if you would hold up your end of the bargain and transport me to a good English prison? Somewhere where fog is just fog, and the dead stay dead, and the only things walking about on two legs are men? Please, your lordship?

You promised, milord! You promised!

Chapter Four

August 17, 1743

To: Admiral Archibald Buchanan, HMS Lionheart

Addendum

Admiral,

Though I have already taken disciplinary action against Sergeant Black, the man charged with transcribing Carpenter's confession, I fear some investigation must be made of my crew and its officers. Despite my personal command to keep the pirate's wild tale in the strictest confidence, the sergeant appears to be one who likes to tell tales with his drinking companions, and within two days of its making, Carpenter's confession was common knowledge with the superstitious crew. It was brought to my attention that many sailors and—though it pains me to admit it—even some of my officers made their way to the cells to hear bits of the tale from Carpenter himself.

I was just ordering Captain of Marines Tobias to go down and take charge of the situation when the crow called a fog warning. Before I could make my way onto the deck a dense sea fog rolled in, reducing visibility to a mere twenty yards and, coincidentally, of a peculiar and foul odour. Already primed by the repetitions of Carpenter's tale, the more superstitious of the crew began to panic, crying that they didn't sign on to fight island demons. Captain Tobias and myself moved to restore order and were mainly successful until interrupted by faint shrieks coming from the cells.

Captain Tobias and I made our way belowdecks only to find Carpenter's cell empty, the door obviously forced. I called for an all-hands search of the ship, but of Carpenter there was no sign. The fog persists, even thickens, making the search more difficult, but the search does continue, though I hold little hope that the prisoner will be found. The state of the cell door indicates to me that rather than escaping, Carpenter was taken, and by more than one man. The only conclusion I can draw at this time is that a mob of crewmen, panicked by the circulating stories and sudden appearance of the fog, did forcibly remove the prisoner from his cell for the purposes of flinging him overboard to assuage the "island demon" they so feared.

I will begin my own investigation immediately, though

with a crew of this size and the number of persons—including officers—who reportedly visited with Carpenter to have his story reinforced, I anticipate ferreting out the culprits in this matter may take some time.

—Hobart Danforth, Captain, HMS Imperious

Chapter Five

August 20, 1743

To: Admiral Archibald Buchanan, HMS Lionheart

Addendum

Admiral,

In the three days since my last written report, nearly half my crew has gone. I initially attributed the missing men to the mania making its way through my ship like a scourge: the belief that Carpenter's demon hides in the fog that still plagues us. The launch boats remain untouched in their berths, however, and I would not have believed that 198 men would individually choose to cast themselves over the side without some sign of land—but there's no sign of anything in this cursed fog that covers the ship. With neither sun nor stars to guide us, I have furled the sails and dropped the sea anchor, letting the current propel us rather than what little breeze we feel in the hopes it may push us into clear air once more.

This fog is like nothing I have ever seen, a damp, clinging cloak thrown over us by some vengeful sea god. The smell of the stuff permeates every corner of the Imperious, *coating each throat with the smell and taste of decay. The constancy of the thing preys upon the mind—even I have thought I heard what sounded like footsteps in the mist, a heavy wood-on-wood tread much as Carpenter described, though I remain aware it is but my imagination coupled with the many times I have sat pondering the prisoner's tale. We must find our way free of the stuff while some small sanity remains in the crew, the officers ... and even myself.*

—Hobart Danforth, Captain, HMS Imperious

~ ~ * * ~ ~

The final report was undated and unsigned, a four-word scrawl barely recognizable as Captain Danforth's hand:

death in the fog

"My God," whispered the admiral. "That's a tale to chill the blood when told by the fireside of a night."

He looked about, surprised; so engrossing was the tale of the *Ravager*, he'd been unaware of the room about him for quite some time. The light, he realized, was nearly gone, the porthole showing but the grey sky of dusk, though he'd have laid good odds it was hours yet until sundown. He slipped around the desk to peer out at the ghost ship before the day was completely gone.

The world on the other side of the glass had been replaced by a grey-white wall of swirling mist. Even through the glass, a faint odour assaulted his nose; he'd inspected the cargo of far too many merchant ships too long at sea not to recognize the scent of spoiled vegetation, though there was something else there, too, something somehow *meaty*...

He spun from the porthole, heart pounding. *The fog's a coincidence, the smell but that story playing with my mind*, he thought, even as he prepared to order the *Imperius* cut free and pushed off as the *Lionheart* got under full sail, visibility be damned.

"Yeoman!"

The door remained closed.

"Smythe! Come in here, man, I need to . . ."

Still the door was closed, no sign of the normally quick-moving Smythe. He glanced to the silvered porthole, then started towards the door, determined to carry the order himself if he had to. "Smythe! Damn you, man, have you fallen aslee—"

As his fingers touched the knob, there was finally a sound from the passageway beyond. Admiral Buchanan froze as a tendril of evil-smelling mist wove its way beneath the door, and he heard a heavy, wood-on-wood thud. And then another. And another. Like ponderous foot-steps moving through the fog in the corridor, drawing closer to his unlocked door.

GRAVE MARKER

EZEKIEL KINCAID

THE MEMOIR OF DARIUS FISCHER

The Memoir of Darius Fischer
by
Dr. Brevard Shaw

"It has now been ten days since his passing, and I must write in order that what has happened and is happening may not be forgotten."

–Darius Fischer

The following is a compilation of the journal entries of Darius Fischer, along with the documentation of my sessions with Mr. Fischer. Included also are details of my own experience and facts from the police reports.

Because the world needs to know…

Darius Fischer, 01 October 1910

My grandfather was an odd man. One so odd that it was most difficult to tell if he was an absolute loon or an absolute genius. My siblings and I were intrigued by him. He was an authentic Native American, and his many stories of ancient spirits and the recounting of great wars fought by his ancestors entertained us for hours when we were children. I spent many an evening listening to him pontificate on such subjects. Talkative though he was, he was also a man of many secrets. Something I was suspicious of but didn't know for certain until after his death.

Four days ago, I traveled to my grandfather's home in the mountains of Boone, North Carolina. His house is a quaint, rustic place that looks like it was transplanted there from Scotland. The doors were solid oak and looked as if they belonged on a tavern or dungeon rather than a house. The house itself is almost entirely stone; gray and white cobblestone with arched windows and castle-like roofing.

My grandfather kept all the things that were important to him in the loft. It was his special place. To me, it was a foreboding place: dark and dingy, and cold in the winter time. The pale lighting caused imp-like shadows to lick across the wall like mist seeping out of a crypt. In this room, he sheltered his many ancient Indian artifacts—totem poles, shaman necklaces, spears, rugs, and talismans. The totem poles were put in the two tall corners of the loft, while the rest of the artifacts were hung on the wall and the arch. In one corner, he had a pile of stuffed chimeras. The way they were piled one each other made them look as though they had mutated and melded together to form another, more insidious creature. In the middle of the room was a desk, and off to the side, in the other corner, there was a chest. In this chest lay all the secrets. All the suspicions of my childhood were housed there.

When we were young, we knew something of grave significance rested in that box of wood and brass. Every time we entered the loft, my grandfather's eyes would turn to that chest, and then back to us, and then back to the chest again. Almost as if he was making sure we kept our distance, and we did. He had warned us to keep away, and our fear was greater than our curiosity. I had always stayed clear from that chest.

As I walked up the spiral staircase, each stepped creaked, as if warning me to turn back. I gave the loft door a slow push, holding my breath at the all-too-loud squeal of its hinges, and peered into the gloom. The light from my candle danced upon the walls, showing me nothing had changed. It was just like I remembered it when I was younger—the totem poles, artifacts…everything, even the chest. That damned chest. It seemed to glare at me, as if what was inside was beckoning me to release it from its years of imprisonment.

I approached the chest and observed that the lock had remained untouched. At that moment, a memory from my childhood surged forward. My grandfather used to keep an old music box on the top right corner of his desk. Inside that music box was the key to his chest. The music box was black, lined in silver, and played *The Wolf is Out!* by J. Arnold Esq. I vaguely remember the song as a child. The first line went,

"Arm broth-ers arm! The Wolf the Wolf is out,
The Coun-try's up and the Bow-men shout."

I didn't understand it then, but even so, that song sent chills down my spine when I was a child.

I walked towards the desk and noticed that the music box was still there. I paused, took a deep breath, and opened it. The tune played, and the words went through my head again…

"Arm broth-ers arm! The Wolf the Wolf is out,
The Coun-try's up and the Bow-men shout."

It had the same effect on me as it did when I was a child.

The music box had a small drawer in it. I pulled it open, hoping that its contents remained. I was not disappointed. The brass key shimmered in the candlelight. I awoke it from its sleep and snuggled it into the palm of my hand.

I walked over to the chest, knelt beside it, and blew the dust off the top. The rising dust floated in front of the candle, and for a moment, it reminded me of the old, grainy, photo that my grandmother took of my grandfather sitting at his desk.

I turned the key and opened the chest. Confusion came over me as I gazed upon its contents. Strands of grayish-white hair tied together with a thin piece of leather. What? Such a big chest for such a small treasure? What could have been so important about some strands of hair? Why was he hiding this in here for all these years? Why did he forbid us to see it? These were just a few of the questions that were going through my mind as I held the strands closer to the candlelight.

In the morning, I checked my coat pocket to make sure the strands of hair were secure, then I kissed my grandmother goodbye and returned to my home in Asheville.

Darius Fischer, 03 October 1910

There were strange occurrences last night in my home. I was awakened from my sleep just after midnight. The moonlight gleamed through my window as if it were searching for whatever had awoken me. I followed its rays to my bedroom door, which was now open. In the doorway, I noticed a large, shadowy figure, whose eyes seemed to reflect the moonlight right back at me. It raised its arm and pointed at me. I lit a candle as fast as I could. The figure was gone. I searched the house but found no figure and no sign of entry or disturbance.

With much effort, I was able to find sleep again. What awaited me in dreamland would make a man wish he would never slumber again.

In my dream, I saw totem poles lain on the ground in the formation of a pentagram. The poles were on fire, and the shadowy figure that I saw in my doorway began to form from the smoke that was rising from the fire. His mouth opened to reveal sharp, dog-like fangs, and he lunged toward me with a snarl, then disappeared. Following this apparition arose a beast of fire that walked within the pentagram.

The shadow figure re-appeared behind me. He grabbed hold of me and threw me into the burning pentagram. The fire beast then held me down as the shadow figure hovered over me. The shadow figure stared at me with his moonlit eyes, and then it opened his mouth to devour me. At that moment, I awoke in a cold sweat.

I looked down and saw burn marks on my arm.

Darius Fischer, 04 October 1910

Last night, I was awakened by the sounds of screaming and growling. I looked out my window and saw nothing. I lit a lamp and explored the premises, but all was quiet.

I went back to my room to find sleep. I blew my lamp out and rolled over on my back to get comfortable. I closed my eyes, only to be awakened again by a fierce jolt. When I opened my eyes, the shadowy figure was hovering over me. His faced pressed against my face, his moonlit eyes staring into mine. I was paralyzed with fright. He growled and snarled, and then it seemed as though I absorbed him. In that same moment, I saw the fire beast dripping through my ceiling like one large raindrop of fire.

Darius Fischer, 05 October 1910

The content of my dreams has been quite alarming. I ventured to talk to my fiancée, Elizabeth, today. She seemed unconcerned and told me that I am probably internalizing the pain that I feel from my grandfather's passing. Regardless, an evening with her was much needed. I found great comfort in her presence. Her voice is calming, like the trickling of a brook as it pours over the rocks. When we were done conversing, I kissed her goodnight, ran my hand through her wavy black hair, and bid her farewell.

Darius Fischer, 07 October 1910

I haven't seen the shadow figure in a few nights, nor have I had the nightmare again. However, yesterday, I blacked out and couldn't account for three hours of my afternoon. When I awoke, I was curled up naked in my outhouse.

It now seems as if I am suffering from somnambulism. Last night, I awoke naked in the field of the Lambert's farm. Five miles from home, how? I am thinking of going to talk to a psychiatrist. Has my grandfather's death impacted me far more than I would like to admit? Maybe Elizabeth is right.

Darius Fischer, 08 October 1910

The events of last night have convinced me that I am indeed in need of a psychiatrist. I awoke again, only this time in an unfamiliar place—the woods, which I would later discover were the ones three miles behind my house. As the weariness began to leave my body, I noticed I was covered in blood, and it was not mine. What happened? What did I witness? What did I do!?

I sat down and began to recount my recent experiences. I observed that these events began right after I returned home from my grandfather's house. There seems to be some connection between the strands of hair and the odd occurrences as of late. I then pulled the strands of hair from my nightstand and examined them. Connection? It's possible. At this point, I need some answers and am willing to explore every avenue. I need to get in touch with my grandmother and go back to Boone for another visit. I must also speak to Elizabeth about these strange connections. I am also going to contact a psychiatrist when I get back in town.

Darius Fischer, 09 October 1910

Today, Elizabeth came over, and I finally told her about the connectedness of all these strange events. She was cordial, but I could tell she was starting to become worried about my sanity. When I revealed to her the hairs, she stopped her talking mid-sentence. Her hand reached for the hairs with an air of caution. She examined the hairs with care, and then laid them down on the table. I then broke down and cried as I explained to her in detail about my blackouts and waking covered in blood.

She placed my head upon her breast and caressed my hair with gentle strokes. I now believe her worry has become angst. I think she understands that something is going on that neither of us feels prepared to handle. She urged me to see a psychiatrist, and I assured her that I would the moment I returned from Boone.

Darius Fischer, 10 October 1910

Today, I recounted to my grandmother the strange occurrences of the past week and a half, and she seemed very concerned for me. She agreed that I needed to see someone. I told her that I needed to search through grandfather's things. I did not tell her about the strands of hair I took from the chest.

I walked up the spiral stairs to my grandfather's loft and entered that wretched room again. This time there was no intrigue or mystery, but terror; disdain. When I saw the totem poles, I went limp and hit the ground. Images of my nightmare began to flash through my mind. After a few moments, I regained my composure. I knew the answer would lie somewhere in my grandfather's desk.

While perusing through the desk drawers, I found a brown leather satchel. I opened it and discovered three sheets of paper. What was written on them struck me as the most important and terrifying words I would ever read.

The first thing I noticed was the drawing of a pentagram. This pentagram was made of totem poles. As I began to read further, I felt as if I were dreaming again. The paper spoke of an old Indian Shaman named Shon'-ge-sab-be, or "Black Wolf." The Shaman was given this name because of the spirit that possessed him. The paper stated that upon the Shaman's death, the spirit was released. The spirit would return and possess the poor soul who removed the sacred strands from their resting place.

The papers also reported that Shon'-ge-sab-be was a shapeshifter. He would turn into a man-wolf and prowl the night. I slammed the papers down on the desk and chuckled. Could this be real? The Native-American version of werewolves? Oh, come now! I picked the papers back up and read on. The hairs that were bound together were reported to be from a white werewolf, a gray werewolf, and a black werewolf. The black being from Shon'-ge-sab-be. As I continued, I was informed that the Shaman was my grandfather's great-grandfather, and that the hairs have been passed down from generation to generation. It was the request of the Shaman, and no Native-American goes against the request of a Shaman. Here these strands have remained undisturbed for generations, until now.

This is why grandfather did not want us to have the hair. It was dangerous—in his mind anyway. Is what I have been experiencing the curse of the "Black Wolf"? The shadowy figure, is he the demon of the "Black Wolf"?

My better judgment got a hold of me. This is Native-American superstition. This is preposterous. After all, I am a rationalist, a naturalist. The supernatural is a figment of the imagination; a projection of weak and diluted souls; folklore, superstition. But I could not deny the events that happened to me. They were real. Maybe a psychiatrist will have the answer.

Darius Fischer, 12 October 1910

I met with a psychiatrist today. Dr. Reems. He was a pleasant man and seemed to listen with great interest. I told him everything—the hair, the nightmares, the blackouts, and the sleepwalking. The only thing he seemed concerned about was me waking covered in blood. Since there have been no murders reported, he seemed assured that I took out my suppressed anger on a poor, helpless animal. He told me that since I was close to my grandfather, it is not odd that I would be dealing with my grief this way. He assured me that it would pass and wants to continue meeting with me, to make sure that I cease in directing my emotions toward helpless creatures. He also wants me to be honest about my feelings of losing my grandfather. The nightmares of the shadowy figure were probably just suppressed memories of my childhood. He is sure that at some point, my grandfather told me about these things, but I didn't remember. It took his death to bring all these things out of my subconscious into my cognitive memory, and it was happening through dreams. He also told me not to be alarmed by the hair or the papers; they were all Native-American and religious nonsense. I agreed.

I talked with Elizabeth about my session with Dr. Reems today. She seemed relieved that it went so well and was happy that we found an answer to what ails me. Our conversation then turned to our wedding plans. As we talked, I realized how deep my love for this woman is. A rare jewel is she. She has my heart, and I have hers.

Darius Fischer, 13 October 1910

I have been having more blackouts, and my somnambulism continues. Last night, I ended up ten miles away from my home. But that is not the disconcerting part. What troubles me is that I woke up naked in a cow pasture, covered in blood. I was surrounded by cows that had been shred to pieces. My immediate thought—Dr. Reems is wrong.

Darius Fischer, 14 October 1910

One of the things I have not relayed yet is the extreme pain and soreness that I have been experiencing over the past month, especially after one of my "blackouts." At first, it was bearable, but after last night, the pain has intensified to so great a degree that I find it difficult to carry out my daily tasks. My bones ache, my body is sore, and my entrails feel as if someone has been rearranging them. I have been vomiting, urinating, and passing blood all day. I called in to the town doctor, but he cannot figure out what is wrong with me. He suggested that I take an extended leave from work for both mental and physical health reasons. I will heed his advice.

Darius Fischer, 14 October 1910

I decided I would converse with my friend, Winston Blanchard, a priest in training. The fact that we are friends is quite ironic. I am a naturalist, who sees no need for a god, while he is a priest. Yet despite our differences, we are close. I guess it is his "pastoral" demeanor, but I feel as if I can be myself around him and tell him anything.

Winston hung on my every word. He seemed convinced that I was not crazy and that what I was experiencing was not a result of grief. He, being Catholic, saw the source of my grandfather's religion as demonic and warned me that what I was dealing with could be very dangerous. I agreed that what was happening was dangerous, and told him I would consider his claims of demonic activity (I am aghast that I am even considering this).

He then began to talk with me about lycanthropy. I stopped him right there and forbade him to speak any further. Demons I can tolerate, but lycanthropy? I know what has happened. I know what my grandfather wrote down. But I cannot accept it. I bid him farewell and returned to my home. Oh, it bears mentioning that I never returned to see Dr. Reems. Though I might not have agreed with Winston, I knew that what was happening was more than just grief.

Darius Fischer, 15 October 1910

Last night, I had another "episode." When I awoke, I was lying naked in the sitting room of someone's home; again, covered in blood. Panic struck me and fear seized me. It took me a few moments to gather myself. I called out, but no one answered. So I arose, obtained a throw from off the sitting room sofa, and exited the room.

I called out again, but no answer. I roamed the kitchen—no sign of life. I walked back out past the sitting room and turned to go up the staircase. My breath left me as if I had been punched. Blood splatters christened the wall and the steps. There were also footprints in the blood, but the footprints were not human. They were more animal-like.

When I reached the top of the stairs, I called out again; still no answer. For some strange reason, I began to feel great infirmity in my stomach. I had the premonition that I was about to witness something atrocious.

I turned towards the master bedroom. One door had been ripped off its hinges, while the other looked like the middle of it had been shredded. As I entered the bedroom, I fell to my knees. What once seemed like it was a white room now had tones of crimson. Two things that resembled humans decorated the furniture: one in the bed and the other strewn across the nightstand.

I left the room and staggered down the hall. I came across another room with its door tattered as well. At first, I refused to go in, but then curiosity got the better of me. Out of respect, I will not dare recount the detail of what I encountered in that room. Who could do that to children? I wish I never would have entered that room.

I continued to roam the house looking for clues to whom or what might have done this. I found no weapons but noticed that the sitting room window was broken. At that moment, I realized my current state and decided that I needed to exit the premises before anyone arrived.

How I returned home without anyone noticing me is still beyond my comprehension. It was around 4 a.m. by the time I arrived at my abode. At first, I did not recognize the house that I awoke in, but it was only two miles off the main road and four miles from my home. After I washed and could compose myself, I remembered just whose house that was. It was the Baukham family. Jonathan, the husband, owned the local bank. He was married to Joanna; his two children were Tabitha and Edward. I just had breakfast with Jonathan last week.

Upon this revelation, I was confused, angry, distraught, afraid, and myriads of other emotions filled me. The police were not sure what to make of the scene, and the best they could come up with was an attack from a rabid black bear. A manhunt was then assembled to track and find this bear in order to dispose of it. They said that what was done to the Baukham family could not have been accomplished by a human being.

But I knew better. Somehow, I knew that I had done it. It was just like the animals I killed, but more severe, more violent, more brutal. But the carnage? How? How was it possible? These people were ripped to ribbons?

Could the Shaman be right? No, it cannot be! It defies reason! But how else can all this be explained? He must be right. Nothing else can account for this. I am a reasonable, logical man, and though I might not like where the evidence is pointing, it is pointing towards lycanthropy. There is only one way to find out. Tomorrow I will contact Winston and see if he is open to discussing things further.

Darius Fischer, 16 October 1910

I have decided to refrain from telling last night's experience to Elizabeth. I thought it better not to worry her, seeing that she is already so concerned for my welfare. Rather, I confided to Winston about what happened. I have informed him of my experiences and all that I have been feeling. He seems convinced that the source is demonic. I reluctantly asked him about performing an exorcism, and he refused. He said that it is something that the Church must approve and that there was no way that they would approve a seminary student to do such a task.

After much pleading, he gave in. He warned me that I mustn't tell a soul what we were up to or he would suffer great consequences. He said that it was not wise to do such a thing alone and that he might have three seminary friends that would be interested in helping. At this point, I am not bothered by who comes. I just want to be free. We decided to meet at an old, abandoned farmhouse 10 miles outside of town tomorrow at 10 a.m.

Darius Fischer, 17 October 1910

If words could be weighed by their emotions and feelings, mine would outweigh the world. The emotion in which I write tonight cannot be relayed in mere narrative or prose. Oh, to see what I have seen and to feel what I have felt! Words will not do justice to what I witnessed today. I am the only one living who will be able to relay it. Well, pieces of it.

The dreary old barn seemed to have been expecting us. It was as if it had been waiting all its existence to house the evil events that were about to transpire. As we walked inside, the sunlight peeked through the cracks between the boards to add to this aboding feeling.

The only things in the barn were piles of hay, a chair, and a strait-jacket. Winston introduced me to his three friends, but I cannot recall their names. I was too nervous. Winston told me not to be alarmed by the straitjacket. He said it was for all our safety. He said that possessed people often show superhuman strength and that it was just a precautionary measure. I assured him that I was fine with it. After what I have seen, I need to be constrained.

They prayed with me, sat me in the chair, strapped me in the jacket, and then tied me to the chair with a rope. Winston pulled out a satchel and opened it. Its contents consisted of holy water and a crucifix. A beginner's exorcism kit I presumed. I relayed this to Winston, and he laughed.

My recollection of what happened next is very vague. Winston began to mutter something over me in Latin, threw holy water on me, and pulled out the crucifix. Nothing happened. Again, he quoted some prayers from some exorcism saint, said some more in Latin, and presented his crucifix. Nothing happened. Then he began to command the demon in the name of Jesus to manifest itself. He said, "The power of Christ compels you!" Again, nothing happened.

I began to get agitated and started to curse Winston and told him this was all nonsense. Then, as a last resort, he pulled out his holy bible. At that moment, something seized me. I began to get dizzy. My last memory is Winston quoting 1 John 3:8, "For this purpose the Son of God was manifested, that he might destroy the works of the devil."

Next, it was like I was having a vivid dream. I felt strange sensations all over my body. I lost control. Something more powerful than me seized all my faculties. I remember extreme pain all over and feeling as if I were being turned inside out. I overcame my restraints and lunged towards Winston. That is all I remembered until I awoke.

When I regained consciousness, I surveyed my surroundings and remembered where I was and why I was there. I was naked and covered in blood. I saw the carnage of the scene and started to vomit profusely as I discovered that I was wallowing in a pile of entrails.

Oh, my friend, my precious friend Winston. Such a loyal friend; all he wanted to do was help, and he paid for it with his life. At this point, I knew it was real. So I screamed.

Darius Fischer, 18 October 1910

Today, I contemplated turning myself in to the police. Maybe a jail cell would contain me? I feel lost; hopeless; guilty. I am a murderer. A monster. A freak. I feel as if at any moment I could become lost within this thing for eternity. For so long I have had disdain for the supernatural and for religion. I saw it as an unnecessary myth for deluded, irrational people. But this is real. This is something beyond the realm of the natural. No psychotic illness can cause a man to do what I did with my bare hands. It is not humanly possible. Dear God, if you are real. I need help.

Elizabeth came calling for me, but I ignored her pleas. I cannot face her. I cannot face anyone right now. What would I say to her? Confess that I am a murderer? What of our relationship then? She is the love of my life. I cannot lose her. I will talk to her tomorrow, after I regain some composure.

As I pondered the events of yesterday, I was perplexed as to why none of the ritualistic chants and mantras that Winston uttered had any power in conjuring up the evil within me. These were Catholic rituals that have been used in the Church for ages. Why no response? Why was it that the sight of a bible put things into motion? Why did Winston reading out of it cause this thing to surface? Furthermore, for the first time, why did I remember some of what happened? These are questions I need answers to.

Darius Fischer, 19 October 1910

In the afternoon, I spoke with Elizabeth. She inquired as to why I did not answer her when she came to the house, and I told her that I was not feeling well and was in a deep sleep. She could tell that I was not being completely honest with her. I tried to assure her that all is well and that I was just a bit under the weather. With reluctance, she accepted my story and offered to stay and cook dinner for me.

Darius Fischer, 20 October 1910

No nightmares last night. Elizabeth's presence seems to have a calming effect on me. However, it now seems that I am hallucinating while I am awake. Earlier this evening, Elizabeth and I attended a party at the Anderson's. I agreed to go, but with great reluctance. My body aches, but Elizabeth thought it would do me good to spend a night out.

While we were at the Anderson's, all conversing in the parlor, I strolled by the bar to get another drink. As I did, I happened to glance at the mirror. Instead of my reflection, I saw the shadow beast. It was ever so quick, but it was enough to startle me. I shook it off and went about my business. About forty-five minutes later, while I was sitting on the sofa enjoying a bourbon, I caught something out of the corner of my eye. As I turned to see what it was, I saw a beast walking on two legs headed straight toward me. I looked at the table to set my drink down, but when I looked up, it was gone.

Curiosity got the best of me, so with great effort, I lifted myself off the sofa and wandered around the house looking for this beast. As I turned the corner and headed into the dining room, I saw the beast. He was standing right behind where Mrs. Anderson was sitting. The beast moved its claws in slow motion and placed them on the head of Mrs. Anderson. He then crept them down the sides of her ears, then to her neck, then to her shoulders. The beast looked at me with an air of satisfaction, then pressed her shoulders and bit down on her neck.

Blood exploded forth like a geyser. The beast then ripped her head off and set it on Mr. Anderson's plate. I let out a deafening scream. As I did, the entire table turned and looked at me, bewildered. I looked at Mrs. Anderson. She was there, unharmed, and was gawking at me like I had gone mad. Indeed, I have.

Elizabeth ran to the room and escorted me out. On our way home, she apologized for pressuring me into this. I told her not to worry and that I knew she was trying to help. I assured her of my love for her, and how precious she was to me, and how I appreciated her trying to help. When I arrived at home, I was so tired and in so much pain that I went right to bed.

Darius Fischer, 21 October 1910

Dear God, what am I becoming? This morning I awoke while it was still dark outside, except I wasn't in my bed. Like the times before, I was naked and covered in blood. As I picked myself up off the floor, I wiped the blood from my eyes so that I could get a better view of where I was. The first thing I noticed was a white curtain, which had been shredded. I began to walk and stepped on something sharp. As I looked down, I saw that the floor was covered with broken glass and china. I reached to my left and felt something hard, like a table. I waved my hands around in the dark and found a chair. I pulled the chair out and flung myself into it. My eyes were starting to adjust in the darkness, and I saw a lamp sitting untouched in the middle of the table. I grabbed the lamp and lit it with the matches that were lying next to it. As I brightened the lamp, I saw Mrs. Anderson, decapitated, and her head was lying in her husband's plate. I am not sure where Mr. Anderson was, but by the looks of it, it appears he was everywhere.

When I arrived home, I washed myself and then sat in a chair and stared at the wall the entire night. I must tell Elizabeth.

Darius Fischer, 22 October 1910

Today, I did not attempt to leave my home, knowing that the police would be about today. I invited Elizabeth over to confess to her, but when she got here, I found myself unable to talk to her. She pleaded with me in tears to tell her what was going on. When I could not bear to see her crying any longer, I opened up.

When I finished, she said not a word; she embraced me and confessed her love for me. She promised she would not leave me but would help me through this. I still think she does not believe that I killed the people that I say I have. Rather, I suspect that she thinks I am just going mad.

Darius Fischer, 25 October 1910

This afternoon, Elizabeth came over. We held each other and danced to imaginary music. My joints and bones ached, but the feeling of her pressed up against me made me lucid. To hold her in my arms and drink the passion from her lips, it made the pain dissipate, even if it was for a brief time. Even now, the pain in my hands and arms is unbearable. So much so, that it is becoming a chore just to write.

As we were dancing, I was admiring our love in the large mirror that hung in my sitting room. I looked back at Elizabeth and turned her head towards the mirror. We laughed at ourselves and then resumed our dancing. In my moment of bliss, I turned my gaze towards the mirror again and saw that Elizabeth was not dancing with me, but with the beast. It grabbed her throat, lifted her off the ground, and stuck its claw in her chest. The beast pulled out her heart, ate it, and then ripped her in half and threw her in two pieces to the ground. "You are the death of her!" it growled.

I screamed and fell to the ground. I came back to reality upon hearing Elizabeth yelling my name. I warned her that she must go and that she must stay as far away from me as possible. She was crying and wailing as I pushed her out the door.

I went to my closet and pulled out my rifle, loaded it, and stuck the barrel in my mouth. Then for some odd reason, right before I pulled the trigger, my mind turned to Dr. Reems again. There were several doctors who practiced at his office. I had chosen Dr. Reems because of his naturalistic leanings and presuppositions. I did not want anyone religious examining me. I recalled that there was a man who practiced there named Dr. Brevard Shaw, who used to be a Presbyterian pastor. He obtained a double Ph.D. from the University of Edinburg in the areas of psychology and theology.

For some reason unbeknownst to me, I had an overwhelming sense that I needed to talk to this man. So, I put the gun down and decided I would make an appointment.

Dr. Brevard Shaw: Case notes for case 00217 (Darius Fischer). Session 1, 28 October 1910

Mr. Fischer complains of blackouts in which he has no recollection of where he has been or what he has done during this time. The blackouts last between three and four hours.

He claims he has committed unspeakable acts during these blackouts but has no proof other than what he sees when he awakes.

He believes he is demon possessed.

Mr. Fischer recounted the events that transpired between 01–27 October 1910. He states he found strands of werewolf hair in a trunk in his grandfather's loft a few days after his grandfather's passing. He also claimed to have found three pieces of paper which give an account of a curse from a Shaman that has been placed upon the person who disturbs the werewolf hair from its resting place.

Mr. Fischer complained about nightmares in which he saw a black, shadowy figure and then claimed to have become possessed by this black figure. He also claims hallucinations of a black beast.

He claims that this demon transforms him into a werewolf.

He also claims that this demon taunts him, revealing to him who his next victims will be.

He claims that he was the one who murdered the Baukham and the Anderson families, along with four seminary students.

He claims that this demon wants to kill his fiancée, Elizabeth, next.

I will investigate these claims further, but I highly doubt he is responsible for the Baukham and Anderson murders. What was done to them was humanly impossible. As far as the seminary students go, I will visit the barn this afternoon to see if he is telling the truth.

As to his claims of demon possession, I will take them seriously and investigate further.

As to his claims of lycanthropy, I will be more cautious. Indeed, it may be that he has clinical lycanthropy (believing himself to be a werewolf). Such episodes are usually triggered by tragic events such as the loss of a loved one, in which the one in grief believes he must change in some type of way to deal with the loss.

However, I am also familiar with claims of mythical lycanthropy. During my travels to Africa, a few of the Ugandan tribes testified to having witnessed a man change into a tiger. Again, on a mission trip to Brazil, some of the locals testified to having seen a man transform into a jackal. There is also the well-documented case of Dr. Jaques Dubious from France, who, when exploring the new world, came across a Native American tribe. During one of the rituals to their great spirits, he witnessed the Shaman transform into a wolf-like creature.

Thus, given Mr. Fischer's connection to the dark spirits of this Native American shaman, I will investigate his claim, though with caution.

Dr. Brevard Shaw, Journal Entry, 28 October 1910

Today I had a most disturbing case. A Mr. Darius Fischer came by to speak with me. He believes he is possessed by a demon that transforms him into a werewolf. The poor man seemed vexed beyond measure and longed for help. He seemed so lost and without hope. He recounted to me how he used to be a naturalistic, rationalist atheist. Now he claims that he believes in the supernatural and is willing to believe in whatever god will rescue him from his malady.

The man seems as though he has a cloud of sinister darkness behind his eyes, just waiting to come out. I must confess that I felt a great disturbance in my spirit when he was recounting his experiences with me. I want to help this man if I am able. Dear Lord, give me the strength and wisdom to minister to this man and show him the superiority of Christ. I have dealt with demonic possession several times before and will be taking the time over the next few days to determine whether this man is demon possessed or just psychologically disturbed.

Also, I went to visit the barn where Mr. Fischer claimed to have murdered those students and found nothing. No hint of blood, no body parts, and no sign of a disturbance.

Dr. Brevard Shaw: Case notes for case 00217 (Darius Fischer). Session 2, 29 October 1910

Today I confronted Mr. Fischer about the state of the barn and the absence of anything that remotely resembled a murder. He seemed genuinely shocked and taken back. He was speechless for a few minutes and seemed as though he had trouble processing the information I just presented to him. He began to cry and said he didn't understand. I also told him that no one has been reported missing as of yet.

I relayed to him that I was able to obtain access to a police report concerning the Baukham and Anderson families, and from what I saw in the reports, no human could have accomplished it. He replied that the reason was because a human did not do it, a werewolf did.

I asked him again about his blackouts, and he claimed that he cannot remember what takes place during these times. He then informed me as to why he was with the seminary students he claimed to have murdered—an exorcism. He claimed that one of them, Winston, began to perform the standard Catholic rites of exorcism on him to no avail.

Then, Winston pulled out a Bible and began to read from it. At this point, Mr. Fischer claims to have remembered feeling himself transform into the werewolf and remembers himself lunging at Winston. That is all. His next memory is waking up in a pool of entrails.

I believe there is a connection between his grandfather's death, the strands of hair, the nightmares, the shadow figure, the hallucinations, and the lycanthropy. The demonic dreams and visions, along with the great aversion to Scripture, cause me to take the claim of demonic possession more serious than I did at first. In all other respects, Mr. Fischer seems like a normal, stable individual with no history of psychiatric illness prior to this event. I also find it extremely unconvincing that one in the circumstances of Fischer would have had such an adverse reaction to losing his grandfather. Though he was close to him, he had not spoken to him in six years. This was due to his grandfather's extreme case of dementia. This is something more than grief, much more. I will commence with the initial stages of an exorcism to see if anything will surface.

He also mentioned that he had done a session with Dr. Reems. I talked with Reems today and chided him for his stupidity.

Darius Fischer, 29 October 1910

I have been meeting with Dr. Brevard Shaw for the past two days. He seems to be both an educated and compassionate man. He seems concerned about my plight and my wellbeing. He listens and doesn't treat me like I am mad.

I am confused over what Dr. Shaw relayed to me yesterday concerning the incident in the barn. No bodies? No sign of anything? Very strange. I know I didn't imagine it. I am sure of it. I went by the barn today to check things out, and it was exactly as Dr. Shaw said. Where is Winston? Where are his friends? I went by Winston's today, and he was not home. I believe that is because he is dead. I know I killed him.

My conversation with Dr. Shaw about the exorcism was informative and humorous. I asked him why none of the Catholic exorcism rites worked, and why something seemed to manifest at the reading of scripture, especially one in which Jesus was mentioned as destroying the works of the devil.

Dr. Shaw's answer was both surprising and comical. He told me that the reason the rites didn't work was because they were superstition and that you cannot fight the devil with superstition. He then laughed about my previous naturalistic leanings and my belief of God as being superstitious. He replied, "Superstition, Mr. Fischer? Now Catholicism, that is a religion full of superstition! You were indeed right about that!" I found this quite amusing.

Dr. Shaw proceeded to inform me that the demons are real evil entities that are not moved or intimidated by pieces of wood, water, and Latin utterances. They are especially not intimidated by prayers from dead saints. Rather, demons fear two things: being exposed, and the Son of God. The scripture, relayed Dr. Shaw, exposes the truth of God and the truth about the devil, whereas the Son of God crushes the devil. Jesus has defeated him through his death and resurrection by breaking the power of sin, which gave the devil his power over humanity. When Jesus takes control, the demons must go.

I am not sure what I think of all this religious talk, but it sounds more convincing than what my dear friend Winston both believed and attempted on me. At this point, if this Jesus is real, and if he did do all this, and if he really can set me free, then I hope he proves himself to be. We shall soon see.

Another thing that I found most unsettling is that Dr. Shaw gave me a Bible and marked some passages of scripture for me to read in the gospels about Jesus casting out demons. He wanted to prove to me that what he was talking about was real. When I got home this afternoon, I opened to the first passage marked, began to get dizzy, and then blacked out. When I awoke, the Bible was shredded into pieces and scattered all around my house. The pieces of paper were dripping with urine and feces.

This will be the last I write for some time. My hands are failing me.

Dr. Brevard Shaw: Case notes for case 00217 (Darius Fischer). Session 3, 30 October 1910

Today I attempted to see if there was a demon (or demons) inside Mr. Fischer, with the hopes of performing an exorcism. Upon his request, I agreed to perform the exorcism alone. He did not want to be responsible for the death of any more individuals. He seemed so adamant about it, I acquiesced. Also upon his request, I chained him to his chair. He refused to allow me to attempt an exorcism until I agreed to do this.

After all the preparations, I attempted to agitate the demon in order to get him to manifest himself. Based on Mr. Fischer's previous testimony, I pulled out my Bible and opened it to 1 John 3:8 and read,

"For this purpose, the Son of God was manifested, that he might destroy the works of the devil."

The following is a factual report as to what I witnessed:

Upon my reading of Scripture, Mr. Fischer's eyes glazed over, and his demeanor changed. He began to curse me and my God, and then his voice changed to a deep growl shrouded by a sort of howl.

After this, I saw the plates in his skull begin to separate. His forehead began to slant to an obtuse angle, while his jaw unhinged and proceeded to elongate itself. His nose and lip seemed to merge into one, while his entire face looked as if some invisible force was squeezing his cheekbones together to make it form a narrower shape. His teeth changed right before my eyes into those of a canine. With all these changes came horrendous popping and snapping sounds.

His shoulders began to slant inward, while his elbows seemed to dislocate themselves and then the arms elongate themselves. His fingers grew extremely long, while his nails thickened and evolved into claws. At this point, he broke free from the chains securing his arms to the chair.

His hips also seemed to dislocate themselves and rotate, causing him to come up out of the chair. This rotation turned his buttocks vertical. The upper portion of his legs began to thicken, while the lower part dislocated itself at the knees. Then the lower portion of his legs elongated and reconnected, giving the look of the hind legs of a wolf. While all this was happening, there was an excessive growth of hair over the entire body.

The beast was free, and it was staring right at me. Though I was afraid, I could see fear in its eyes. I tried to speak to it, but it knocked me aside and jumped through my office window and ran off to the woods behind our practice.

Dr. Brevard Shaw, Journal Entry, 30 October 1910

The possession of Darius Fischer is by far the most troubling thing I have ever witnessed in my short 39 years on this planet. His case proves that the myths of lycanthropy are not myths at all, but cases of demonic possession. I was not prepared for this. How can I cast this thing out if its primary manifestation is changing Fischer into a were-wolf? It cannot be contained. If it cannot be contained, it cannot be cast out.

I spent the entire evening in prayer and studying Bible passages on possession. I feel certain that the Lord is telling me that when the demon first manifests itself, I need to command it to not change Mr. Fischer. Also, for extra measure, I will command it not to curse and blaspheme, just to show it who is in charge.

Dear Lord, this is far too much for me to handle on my own. Please grant me the strength to do this. Do not let the evil one have the victory in this. Let it be known tomorrow who is in control and who the rightful ruler of this universe and the Savior of mankind is. Father, glorify your Son.

Dr. Brevard Shaw: Case notes for case 00217 (Darius Fischer).

Session 4, 31 October 1910

When Mr. Fischer entered my office, he could barely walk. It seems as if the transformations are taking a great toll on his body. He has lost weight and looks as if he has aged twenty years.

I assured him that this will all end today. He informed me that he did not want to live anymore. He feels like death is the only way out. I informed him that this is exactly what it wants to do—ruin your life and then destroy you. I asked him for one more opportunity to confront the spirit. He agreed. He asked me if I was going to chain him to the chair, and I informed him that it would not be necessary. Though he did not like this, he was too exhausted to argue with me.

I picked up my Bible, opened it to 1 John 3:8 and read, "For this purpose, the Son of God was manifested, that he might destroy the works of the devil." At that moment, an evil life came into Mr. Fischer's body and caused him to sit up straight. His eyes glazed over and his demeanor changed. Mr. Fischer was gone, and the demon was now present.

The following is my report of the conversation with the demon and the events that transpired during the exorcism.

Demon: I killed those students, and I will kill you, you stupid f…

Shaw: In the name of Jesus, shut your mouth! I bind you from uttering blasphemy and cursing, in the name of Jesus!

(At this point the demon stopped abruptly in its speech and began to growl, snarl, hiss, and howl. Rage and anger filled the face of Fischer

as this demon knew it had to obey.)

Demon: You think you can win, Shaw? I have been doing this for ages, and no one has stopped me. This time shall be no different!

(At this point, the demon attempted to change Fischer into the werewolf.)

Shaw: In the name of Jesus, I command you not to change Fischer into that beast, and in the name of Jesus, I bind you from doing it!

(The demon then let out strange sounds that I can find no words for. My binding him from manifesting the beast and from cursing caused him great torment and vexation. Never have I seen something in this much pain. Never have I seen something with this much hate.)

Shaw: Tell me your name.

Demon: No! You tell me about the whores, Shaw! We all know how you like the whores tickling your little fancy!

(The demon then began to speak in many different languages. Some I recognized, some I did not.)

Shaw: Silence! Since we are talking about my past, let us talk about your future. How you are going to burn in hell forever. And do you think speaking in other languages is going to scare me, demon? I read and speak Hebrew, Greek, Latin, French, German, Spanish, and Russian. Shut up, in the name of Jesus.

Demon: You mock me, human? You are a pest, a disease to be eradicated and destroyed. Your race is weak.

Shaw: You are just jealous because God decided to show us mercy but left you to suffer the consequences of your rebellion. You are an abomination, the offspring of fallen angels and human beings. Now, in the name of Jesus, tell me your name!

Demon: My name is Shon'-ge-sab-be.

Shaw: So, you took the name of the shaman.

Demon: No, fool, the shaman took my name, for I consumed him! And I will consume Fischer, too! You will not have him! You will not take him from me! Destroying him is bringing me great satisfaction. Like your whores, Shaw. Like your whores!

Shaw: In the name of Jesus, shut up! How many of you are there in Fischer?

Demon: One.

Shaw: In the name of Jesus, tell the truth.

Demon: One. You find it hard to believe that one spirit can be this powerful? Indeed, I am. I need no others. None compare to me! I am a devourer, one of the strongest and most faithful to Satan.

Shaw: Like your Master, you are also full of yourself and arrogant to no end. And like your Master, you will suffer defeat, both today and in the final judgment. Your time is up; it is time for you to leave Mr. Fischer.

Demon: No! I will not! You leave, Shaw! You go! Go back to your whores!

Shaw: Let me remind you how this works, demon! I do not obey you; you obey me because I speak as an ambassador of Jesus Christ! In the name of Jesus Christ, come out!
(The demon threw Fischer on the floor and caused him to convulse violently. It began to twist and contort Fischer's body. It screamed and howled with vehemence.)

Shaw: Leave him, in the name of Jesus, and never come back!
(The demon let out one last howl and left. Mr. Fischer's body stopped its violent shaking and became serene.)

The demon had left, and a few moments later, Mr. Fischer awoke. We conversed about what happened, and then I helped him return home.

Dr. Brevard Shaw, Journal Entry, 31 October 1910

On our journey to Mr. Fischer's house, he relayed to me what he remembered about the exorcism. He only remembers the beginning and the end. Like usual, he began to feel dizzy and then blacked out. The next thing he remembered is breathtaking. As he was waking, he told me he saw a Great Warrior wearing a white robe dipped in blood. This warrior had wounds in his wrist and the title "King of King and Lord of Lords" written on his thigh. He was frightened as this Great Warrior drew his sword and stabbed it into him. Yet, once he realized what was happening, he was more mesmerized than afraid.

He told me that as the Great Warrior began to draw back the

sword from his heart, the black shadow figure was on the other end of it. The Great Warrior then took one hand and squeezed the shadow figure around the neck and jerked him out of Mr. Fischer. The Great Warrior then bound the shadow figure with a heavy chain. He also took out a key and unlocked what seemed like a great, dark abyss. The Great Warrior threw the shadowy figure into the abyss, locked the gate, and put away the key.

The Great Warrior then smiled, pulled out a bottle of some sort of oil, and poured it all over him. Mr. Fischer said the oil felt like it was healing the inside of his soul, washing away the guilt, darkness, and pain he had been feeling.

After relaying this story, Mr. Fischer asked me if that was Jesus. I told him yes, it was. He then told me that anyone that powerful, loving, and forgiving deserved to be trusted in.

When we arrived at Mr. Fischer's home, I helped him to his bedroom, left him my Bible, and told him to start reading the Gospel of John. Mr. Fischer thanked me, we shook hands, and I left. That was the last time I would see Mr. Fischer alive.

Postscript:

The next day, a young lady named Elizabeth stopped by my office. She claimed she was Darius's fiancée. She relayed to me that she was aware that he had been seeing me and was concerned for the welfare of Darius. She told me she had been by his home, but no one would answer, and the doors were locked. She asked me to come with her there and check on Mr. Fischer. I hadn't heard from Mr. Fischer either, so I thought it would be a good idea for us to go and check on him. We were able to get in the house, and when we did, we found him dead in his bedroom, with his Bible open to the Gospel of John.

The doctor said that his death was due to severe shock and trauma on his body. I did not tell the doctor what had been occurring with Mr. Fischer, for reasons the reader can understand. That is why this report is being written—to give an account of the events that transpired during the month of October with Mr. Fischer.

I suspect that the transformation into the werewolf, almost every day for close to a month, was too much for the body of Mr. Fischer. After seeing the transformation myself, I am surprised he lasted even a month. The stress on the internal organs must be unimaginable, along with the stress and trauma that the skeleton undergoes during this transformation.

I am now convinced that it was Mr. Fischer who murdered the Baukham and Anderson families, and that he did murder those seminary students. The bodies have not been found, but the four students have been reported missing. I am perplexed over this entire situation and will continue to investigate it. Right now, however, it remains a mystery.

I am confident that Mr. Fischer is present with the Lord now, the Great Warrior who delivered him from so evil an enemy and then brought him safely home to enjoy a paradise and a place that was prepared for him from before the foundations of the world.

Because I am a former clergyman, I will close with this observation. The exorcism happened on All Hallows' Eve, the devil's day. But before 31 October was this, it was Reformation day—the day Martin Luther nailed his *Ninety-five Thesis* to the church door in Wittenberg, Germany. So, how does God take a naturalistic atheist and turn him into a believer? In this case, he used the devil. Therefore, it only seems fitting to close with the words of Martin Luther, "The devil is God's devil."

Soli Deo Gloria,

Dr. Brevard A. Shaw
05 December 1910

ABOUT THE AUTHORS

Barlow Adams is a writer from the Cincinnati area and the author of two novellas and an upcoming horror novel. His poems and short stories have been featured in several not at all creepy magazines, but the creepy ones are secretly always his favorites. Follow him on Twitter @BarlowAdams for scary stories and musings about dumb stuff.

Rob Smales is the author of *Echoes of Darkness*, which garnered both a five-star Cemetery Dance Online review and a 2016 Pushcart nomination. With over three dozen short stories published, his story "Photo Finish" was also nominated for a Pushcart Prize and won the Preditors & Editors' Readers Choice Award for Best Horror Short Story of 2012. His story "A Night at the Show" received honorable mention on Ellen Datlow's list of the *Best Horror of 2014*, while "Death of the Boy" and "In Full Measure" made the same honorable mentions list for 2016. Most recently, he edited the dark humor anthology *A Sharp Stick in the Eye (and other funny stories)* for Books & Boos Press, and released the coming of age horror novella *Friends in High Places* with Bloodshot Books.

Ezekiel Kincaid resides in Baton Rouge, Louisiana, with his wife, four children, and two dogs. When he's not working, writing horror, or doting on his family, he likes to train in martial arts. The only other language he is fluent in is sarcasm. For fun, Zeke enjoys watching people get in socially awkward circumstances. He hates cat videos but loves watching wrestling promos from the 80s.
You can find Zeke over on his blog: https://ezekielkincaid.wordpress.com/
On Facebook at https://m.facebook.com/ezekethefreak/
Or on Instagram at https://www.instagram.com/ezekielkincaid/

Press
Presents

Grave Markers, Volume Five
(includes W.C. Jones's *The Source*, A.P. Sessler's *Brain Attack*, and Andrew Richardson's *The Bathtub*)

Grave Markers, Volume Four
(includes Joseph Rubas's *The Freaks Come Out at Night*, A.P. Sessler's *The First Suitor*, and Neil Davies's *Vampire Worms*)

Grave Markers, Volume Three
(includes Dominic Stabile's *Full Moon in the West*, Adrian Ludens's *Bottled Spirits*, and S.L. Williams's *The Dance*)

Grave Markers, Volume Two

(includes Hal Badner's *Tolerance*, Sebastian Bendix's *Shriek of the Harpy*, and Russell Coy's *The One Who Lies Next to You*)

Grave Markers, Volume One
(includes Richard Black's *Nikolis Cole: the Low-Rise Saint*, Sebastian Bendix's *Rock, Paper, Scissors*, and Joshua Rex's *Coattails*)

www.ingramcontent.com/pod-product-compliance
Lightning Source LLC
LaVergne TN
LVHW010100110826
845155LV00028B/421

* 9 7 8 1 9 4 7 2 2 7 6 6 8 *